Baron

THE K9 FILES

Dale Mayer

BARON: THE K9 FILES, BOOK 25
Beverly Dale Mayer
Valley Publishing Ltd.

ISBN-13: 978-1-778863-22-6
Print Edition

Books in This Series:

Ethan, Book 1

Pierce, Book 2

Zane, Book 3

Blaze, Book 4

Lucas, Book 5

Parker, Book 6

Carter, Book 7

Weston, Book 8

Greyson, Book 9

Rowan, Book 10

Caleb, Book 11

Kurt, Book 12

Tucker, Book 13

Harley, Book 14

Kyron, Book 15

Jenner, Book 16

Rhys, Book 17

Landon, Book 18

Harper, Book 19

Kascius, Book 20

Declan, Book 21

Bauer, Book 22

Delta, Book 23

Conall, Book 24

Baron, Book 25

Walton, Book 26

Boxed Sets and Bundles

https://geni.us/Bundlepage

About This Book

Welcome to the all new K9 Files series reconnecting readers with the unforgettable men from SEALs of Steel in a new series of action packed, page turning romantic suspense that fans have come to expect from USA TODAY Bestselling author Dale Mayer. Pssst... you'll meet other favorite characters from SEALs of Honor and Heroes for Hire too!

The hurricane devastated more than just Baron's world. It hurt so many other people too, including Baron's brother, who died trying to rescue dogs caught up in the storm. One of the missing dogs is a War Dog, Kingston. Now Baron is put on the spot to see if he could find the War Dog again …

Brittany's grandmother's house was destroyed in the hurricane, so Brittany has been searching for her grandmother's little dog, Pocket. When Baron comes to her aid, Brittany remembers her grandmother's warnings about those who take advantage during disasters …

During the aftermath of the hurricane, these two people are looking for missing animals, yet are about to get caught up in the middle of something no one saw coming …

Sign up to be notified of all Dale's releases here!

https://geni.us/DaleNews

B ADGER LOOKED OVER at Kat. "Aren't you tricky?"

She shrugged. "Not necessarily," she said, with a smile, "but it worked out for Bacchus and Michael and Danny and Mariam, plus Conall and Bethany, even her mom and Old Joe. So *two* happy families, and, for that, I'm very happy."

"Now what?" he asked, as he looked at the two files on her desk. "Who are you thinking for the next miracle?"

"I'm not so sure. … This one's a bit trickier."

"Why is that?"

"A hurricane in Florida," she murmured. "The War Dog was on the road with other dogs being transported out of the area. The truck ended up in the river. Details are sketchy, and I might not have this completely right, but it appears the driver, who may have been the transport truck owner, died. Several of the dogs managed to get free and were captured again, but the War Dog is missing."

He stared at her. "A hurricane? Were they in the back of the truck in cages or what?"

"Most were in cages, and some of them were still fine when the truck was found in the river. The cage the War Dog had been in was open, and he is still missing. Several other cages were also open, and those dogs were picked up again, but not the War Dog."

"Where were they taken to?"

"I don't know. As I said, the details are unclear. One guy was airlifted out. I assume he was in the passenger seat of the transport truck. I think he died too, though I'm not certain. The found animals were gathered up by a rescue team and were moved to a safe location," she shared. "And, as for the missing animals, … we don't know any more."

Badger shook his head. "A hurricane."

She nodded. "Yeah, and it happened recently, so a good chance the War Dog is okay, and they have a lot of survival skills. Thus we have a good chance of recovering this one. I do have somebody in mind, but—"

"What's with the *but*?"

She winced. "His brother died in the vehicle."

Badger let out a long whistle. "You're talking about Baron, aren't you?"

She nodded. "I don't know if it's fair to ask him to go after the dog that his brother was trying to rescue."

"On the other hand," Badger pointed out, "better that it wasn't in vain."

She smiled, then nodded. "I was thinking of that as well. I texted him earlier, but I haven't heard back yet."

Her phone rang just then. She looked down and raised one eyebrow. "Speaking of …"

He nodded, anxious to hear how Baron was doing. Kat punched the button to answer.

Baron's voice came through on the other end. "Kat, what's up?"

"Hey, I'm so sorry to hear about your brother."

"Yeah, me too. It's just too awful to imagine."

"Look. I don't know if you heard anything about some of the work we've been doing—"

"Yeah, War Dogs," he interrupted. "My brother was rescuing one."

"Right, and that's one of the reasons I called. I was wondering if you would want to give us a hand."

"What's up?"

"The War Dog is still missing."

"I know. It was in my brother's truck, but I haven't seen or heard anything else about it."

"I guess what I'm asking is, could you track it down?"

"*Right.* That's what you do, isn't it?"

"Yes, we track down War Dogs, but it sounds like maybe your brother had this dog for a while."

"Actually he didn't. He was away for surgery and subsequent rehab. So somebody else was looking after the dog. When he got back home again, the War Dog didn't get returned."

"How did this one end up in your brother's truck then?"

"I don't think we have any paperwork, since everything happened in such a panic with the hurricane," he explained, his voice tired. "Everybody is saying that dog was in the back of the transport, but I don't know if that's really true. Are you sure you want *me* to track down this War Dog?"

"That's what we do," she said. "We find volunteers to get boots on the ground. I realize it's an odd request, since you've just lost your brother, and the area is in such turmoil, and everybody is trying to recover."

"We've got all the people accounted for, but we've got so much clean-up and rebuilding to do to get families housed and businesses restored. On a personal note, I just buried my brother," he added. "Yet you're right. A couple other dogs are still missing, and thankfully they didn't die with my brother. By the way, his death wasn't because of the hurricane itself. Not directly anyway. He'd always had a weak heart valve, and we knew it could fail at any time. He ended up having a heart attack in the process, and that's why he drowned. It wasn't really the hurricane, or even the rescuing of the animals." He took a moment and collected his thoughts. "Any dog that needs a hand, well, I'm just as bad as my brother."

"How's your new foot?"

He laughed. "As always, you were right on target. It's doing better, and I'm becoming more capable with it."

"Good," she replied warmly.

"Okay, fine. I'm game," he said. "Give me a few days to see what I can come up with."

"That sounds good, and again, condolences to you and your family."

"Thank you," he murmured. "Nothing quite like that kind of a loss, but I don't want it to be in vain. He was out helping animals, so I can go help the same animals and ensure the work he was doing gets completed." Baron sighed. "So I'll see what I can come up with." And, with that, he rang off.

Badger looked over at her, one eyebrow raised. "At least he's right there in the area."

"He is, but what happened to the War Dog in the first place sounds a little sketchy to me."

"That seems to be why these cases end up on our desks," he noted, with a tilt of his head. "I don't suppose a ladylove or anything is in Baron's background, is there?"

Kat shrugged and gave him a knowing smile.

Badger narrowed his gaze.

"He did tell me one time that his brother's former wife was first Baron's girlfriend for the longest time. Apparently they broke up at some point, and she hooked up with his brother and married him very quickly afterward. It created a lot of trouble in the family for a long time, including separating the brothers."

"Something like that would surely do it," Badger noted.

"She contacted Baron a while back, and he wouldn't have anything to do with her."

Badger chuckled. "That doesn't mean Baron wants to have anything to do with her now either."

"No, but he might, considering that she tossed off Baron's child as his brother's, only for both of them to find out she never was pregnant."

"Oh, ouch."

She nodded.

"And you really think he'll want anything to do with her after all that?"

"It depends what her reasoning was," Kat suggested. "Who are we to judge? We've all done stupid things in our lives."

He nodded. "Isn't that the truth," he muttered. He walked over, pulled her to her feet, and gave her a big hug. "I do love you. You know that, right?"

"I know you do," she murmured, "and that's a really smart answer right now."

He chuckled, held her close. "You are also incredibly amazing, and I'm so very proud to have you as my partner in this life."

"Ditto," she said, as she pulled him down, gave him a tongue-lashing kiss that had his head swimming. "Now we need to take a break and go for a swim, spending some time with our *kiddos*."

And, with that, she turned and walked out back to the

pool, leaving him watching in awe, as this woman of his joined the other men and their partners who made up the Titanium Corp, making Badger's world complete.

CHAPTER 1

BARON SAGWAY POCKETED his phone and turned to look at his mother, who was slowly moving back and forth on a rocking chair on her deck.

She frowned at him and asked, "Who was that?" He was reluctant to say anything, but she sighed. "I need to know, especially if it involved your brother."

He squatted beside her. "My boss on this job. The one who asked me to look for the War Dog. His wife also designed my prosthetics."

She sniffed, and he knew the tears would follow soon afterward. "The War Dog that Brad rescued?" she asked, her voice low.

Baron nodded. "Yeah, It's one of the animals he rescued," he confirmed, "and I know you may not want to hear it, but we can't blame anybody for what happened to Brad … and certainly not an animal."

Her sniffles continued for a moment, and she finally nodded. "I know that, … in theory." She hung her head. "I mean, it could have happened any day. We knew for a very long time that he had a heart condition that wasn't fixable. Still, it's tough not to consider the idea that, if he hadn't gone out after those dogs, he might still be alive."

"He was also doing what he loved to do, Ma," Baron pointed out, "and I think that's just as important."

She looked up at him. "But he's still gone."

His heart broke at that, and he nodded. "Yes, he is still gone, and nothing will bring him back," he murmured, hating the grief that washed over him. "I know it's devastating, but we can't blame the dogs, and that's the last thing Brad would want us to do."

"I know that." She released a heavy sigh. "It still hurts. I'm glad you two finally buried the hatchet."

"Our issues were a long time ago. A lot of water under the bridge since then and we became close. Very close. You know he was bugging me to come back and move in with him. … So yes, it hurts me too. And it'll keep hurting until we all have a little bit of time to process the loss. It'll hurt forever, but the sadness will get replaced with happier memories. Just because we knew it could happen anytime didn't mean we were prepared and ready for it to happen."

She gave him a ghost of a smile. "You know he would be livid if I even suggested blaming the dog."

"Of course he would," Baron agreed, a smile also lighting his face. "That's who he was."

"Even if you know it to be true, that doesn't mean you have to go running out there and repeat his mistakes."

In the end, that was the crux of the matter. She'd heard just enough of the conversation to realize that Baron could be putting himself in danger to find the dog. "The hurricane is over," he pointed out, "but that dog and whoever else is out there could be in need of rescuing."

Ma shook her head, the soft gray curls bouncing around her head. "God only knows what you were doing for the military, with all your secrets and not even telling your own mother what you did for the government. You lost part of a leg doing your *confidential* work. But that's over, so it doesn't have to be you now," she argued. "I don't care who these people are who are calling you now. I don't care who they send where and what they get themselves into searching for. It doesn't have to involve you."

"No, it doesn't have to be me. However, if it's important to us to complete the work that Brad started, then it needs to be me," Baron stated.

She considered that for a long moment and slowly nodded. "I guess it means his death wouldn't be in vain."

"His death would never be in vain, Ma, not now, … not ever. He spent a lifetime doing all the right things for all the right people, and he made the most out of every day," he declared. "If nothing else, we should be proud of the life he lived."

"I am. Of course I am," she stated crossly, "but that doesn't mean I was ready to let him go. You sit here and preach it, but you know damn well he wasn't ready to go. He was never a quitter."

Baron chuckled. "Not only was he not ready to go, he probably would have laughed at the idea that his time was coming. Still, that doesn't mean we can forget the reality that we all knew it could happen anytime. He understood his situation very well, and he made the decision to live his life to the fullest, and we need to remember that."

She waved her hand dismissively, not wanting to listen to him, but Baron already knew how this would go. Finally she groaned. "At least we're done with the damn hurricane. Will you just look for animals?"

"No, of course not," Baron clarified. "I'll go back over all the places that Brad went to … and see if any of the missing dogs returned to their homes. Plus, I will see if anyone else out there needs help. We haven't had a chance to check on everybody, as it is."

"Which is what Brad was doing too when he died," she muttered.

He nodded. "Yes, exactly. That's when he died."

"Well, then, … I guess you better go out there and see what you can do," she uttered with resolve, "but you better be home for dinner."

He chuckled softly. "This will be my first pass of the area, so I don't know how much time it will take," he explained. "I'm sure that dinner is a reasonable expectation, but it all depends on what we find out there. I know it's not easy for you, but it's not easy for me either."

"We?" she asked.

He nodded. "I'll probably go by the rescue center and see if anybody there is willing to tag along. I'll also need the information on the particular quadrant where it all went down, and help finding my way around, so I'm not just poking around blindly."

She perked up at that. "See? That's what bothers me."

"I understand, but I won't be foolish," he replied, "and I'll let people know where I am. Some areas still aren't as safe as they should be, but I have people who can watch my back."

"Good, it's definitely not as safe as it should be," she noted, glaring at him, "and you know very well I don't want you going at all."

He nodded. "I know that, but you also know I have to go."

"Oh, I know," she grumbled. "Why would you be any different? Your brother had the same attitude."

"When people or animals need help," Baron said, with a smile, "somebody needs to step up. I get that, for you, that doesn't necessarily mean us, but, for a lot of people, *us* is all there is."

She winced. "If your father were here, he would be out there too."

"Of course he would. Where do you think we learned it from?" Baron gave her a smile.

She sighed. "It's still not easy being the one left behind."

"Well, if you were in better physical shape, I would consider taking you with me," he offered. "But, since you aren't, I need you to stay here and to stay safe, while I do what I can to find the animals."

She nodded at that. "You need to stay safe too, son," she declared, looking back at him.

"I will, Ma. I promise."

She rolled her eyes. "You and your brother, you could always roll those lies right off your lips, as if they meant nothing," she replied, "but they need to mean something."

He looked at her and nodded. "I'm not lying. I'll be careful. I promise. Remember that this isn't really connected to what happened to Brad," he added. "You and I both know that his heart event could have happened anytime and anywhere."

She nodded. "I hear you, and I know that, but knowing it and feeling it are two different things."

"Of course. I get it." He leaned over and gave her a gentle hug. "I'll try to be home for dinner, but ..."

"Right, don't wait up," she quipped, with a small smile. "The least you can do is keep in touch."

"That I will do," he promised.

She looked at him intently for a moment and then sighed. "Fine, go on," she relented, waving her hands. "Go find this dog, and, if you find anybody else who's in need, don't forget them either."

"Of course not," he agreed. "I've been doing search and rescue in these types of situations for a long time, so obviously I'll help whomever I can."

"Except," she snapped, "that damn Jolene. Don't you even think of lifting a hand to help that lying gold-digger."

"Jolene?" Baron frowned. "Wow, that's a name from the past. Is she still in town?"

"Of course she is, still looking for another man to believe she's pregnant with his child, just so she can get married and stop working." Ma shook her head. "And to think my two brilliant boys fell for her and her lies is beyond me."

"Now, Ma, we were young and impressionable. However, we learned our lesson. Brad never married again, and he also divorced her as soon as he found out she was not even pregnant." With a final hug, he picked up his wallet, tucked it into his back pocket, grabbed his jacket and his keys, and walked out the door. With any luck, he would make it home for dinner, but it rarely happened, particularly in situations like this.

With a wave from behind the wheel, he pulled out and headed into the devastation where the hurricane had centered. More than one reason to go back there because, in his own mind—and he hadn't mentioned it to his mom and wouldn't if he didn't have more evidence—Baron had this inkling that maybe his brother didn't have to die, and that maybe somebody else's hand had been involved.

Without any proof, Baron had no way to know for sure, which was why working this dog rescue was the perfect cover for him to start digging into what happened to Brad.

BRITTANY STOOD, GROANING as her back screamed at her. Straightening up from the position she'd been in for a long time was always a bitch. She was sorting through things that were salvageable and things that weren't, and it was a never-ending process.

Her grandmother's house had been a really old one and didn't withstand the hurricane's impact. Brittany suspected that the insurance company would write it off as a total loss, and that would just make it even harder on her grandmother. She'd been fighting to stay here instead of going into a retirement home already, and now she couldn't stay here. She was currently over at a friend's, but that was a short-term situation at best.

Brittany walked around the main floor of the house, navigating through the mud and the sand and the garbage that had floated in. Trees had smashed through windows and doors, and, while she knew she wasn't technically allowed to be here, a few other neighbors were wandering through the area, as she was, searching for any valuables that were possible to salvage, though it was looking pretty grim.

Brittany was here because her grandmother was rather desperate for a few things, mostly her little dog, which had been pulled out of her arms, as she had been trying to get out of here. The wind had picked up the little thing and carried her off someplace. Brittany could only hope that someone had found her and she was still alive. If so, she couldn't imagine what the poor little thing might have been through. So Brittany was willing to do whatever was needed to find her and to bring her home. She belonged with her grandmother.

As she did another pass through the place, she thought she heard a little yelp. She froze, tilted her head, and listened again. "Pocket, is that you?" she called out.

She listened intently, thinking she heard another little yelp. She moved quickly in that direction, knowing it wasn't necessarily Pocket by any means, but, if an animal was in need, she was right there for it. She listened again, hearing nothing. Frowning, she wandered through the area and called out to Pocket several more times.

When she heard a vehicle, she stepped back into the shadows. She watched the other neighbors do the same thing. The last time anybody of any authority had come around the area, they had told her to leave because it wasn't safe. Regardless of the buildings still standing, some of those could collapse later—which was a valid observation. Being belligerent about the cops' warnings wouldn't help, and, if those authorities got ugly, she tended to give in. Still, Brittany didn't want to right now, not when potentially she had a sign of progress in finding Pocket.

When the large black truck rumbled slowly down the street, she realized it was likely somebody else looking for people or possessions, or it could also be somebody coming in to take advantage of the situation and steal something. The neighborhood was a mess, with wreckage all over, making it the perfect opportunity to grab other people's stuff and run.

She'd had more than enough of that attitude, and it was hard to fathom. Why would anybody even think to do such a thing when people were already down and out? She didn't know, but more than a few looters had been around the area. The big black truck could only go so far before a tree was in the way.

The driver hopped out, grabbed a chainsaw, and efficiently cut up the tree, pulling it out of the way enough to make room for the truck. She smiled at that, thinking he could come back anytime. She was all for anybody who could make the roads here more accessible.

As the man turned and hopped back into the vehicle, she frowned, thinking it was somebody she knew. She watched carefully, but he didn't appear to recognize her. He did lift a gloved hand and wave, then drove forward. Abruptly he stopped, turned off the engine, and hopped out, walking toward her. She waited. As he got a little bit closer, she realized why he looked familiar, but he wasn't Brad.

He asked her, "Are you okay?"

She shrugged. "I'm looking for my grandmother's dog, … Pocket," she stammered. "Her little dog called Pocket. I wasn't very hopeful, but I thought I heard something a moment ago."

His eyebrows shot up. "Let's give it a good look."

She hesitated. "Do I know you? You look an awful lot like somebody I know."

He looked over at her and nodded. "You're probably thinking of my brother, Brad."

"Yes. I'm surprised I haven't seen him around here."

He hesitated. "You would have," he began, then turned and looked around for a moment, then back at her, "but he passed away."

She froze. "What? Brad died?"

He nodded. "Yeah. He's always had a heart condition, and, doing these rescues, … well, we knew that one day his heart couldn't handle it," he explained. "It's been a pretty rough deal. Sorry to surprise you with that news."

"It's such a shock. I'm so sorry for your loss." She stared at him, stunned. "I had no idea."

He nodded. "Most people don't know. Besides, everyone's got bigger fish to fry right now. Plus it wasn't directly related to the hurricane. His heart just gave out."

"But he still came out and helped everybody anyway," she noted.

He nodded and smiled. "Yeah, he did. That's who he was."

She gave him a warm smile. "Your brother really was an amazing person. If anybody ever needed anything, he was right there."

"And that's good to hear. He was that way as far back as I can remember. He did what he felt was right, but it was hard on our mother. She always worried about him."

"Oh, ouch," Brittany muttered, followed by a sigh. "It's always so hard on those who are left behind."

"What about your grandmother? Is she okay?"

"Well, she's alive," she replied, as she pointed at the devastated house behind her. "This was hers though."

He frowned. "That's pretty ugly destruction."

"It most certainly is. The main structure is still standing, but not a whole lot else. Most of the roof is gone too."

"Will you rebuild?" he asked.

She shook her head. "No, not likely, too much damage. I don't know what her insurance situation is like, but this place was her last wave of defiance to avoid going to a home," she shared, with a small smile. "I'm not sure she'll use that excuse anymore."

"No, but she'll try," he suggested, with a grin. "Is anybody ever ready for that stage in life? I can't say that I blame them."

"I know. Isn't it terrible that we don't have much in the way of other options for them?" Looking around, she shook her head. "I would love to keep her close, but I don't know how to do that now."

He nodded. "Did you know my brother well?" he asked.

She sighed. "Not really. He was always around. I saw him recently, as he was out looking for lost animals. I did ask him if he had seen Pocket, but he hadn't. Apart from that, I don't know where she is, but, a minute ago, I thought I heard a dog." She wandered around and started calling out for her. "Pocket, where are you?"

"Pocket, *huh*? That's an interesting name."

"You should see the size of her," she replied. "She's pocket-size, and that just became her name."

"That's all it takes"—he chuckled—"for nicknames to stick and to become their permanent names."

"Exactly," she agreed. Just then a slight yelp came again. She turned to him excitedly. "Did you hear that?" But he was already striding in that direction. She raced behind him, as he headed around the side of the house. Some roofing was on the ground, with some tree branches on top of it.

He quickly started removing the branches. "Call her again."

She got down to the edge of the roofing and called out to Pocket several more times. When the yelps came again and again, she laughed. "My God, I can't believe it. She's probably under here, isn't she?"

"Maybe." He looked over at her and added, "But ..."

The smile fell off her face. "Right, but that doesn't mean she's in decent shape."

"No, it doesn't, but we don't know either way just yet." He picked up another load of branches. "Let's just stay calm and focus on what we're doing."

And with that good old grim and solid advice, she pitched in to help him move as many of the tree branches as she could. When she bent down to reach for a piece of the roofing, he waved her off.

"You don't have on thick-enough gloves," he warned her. "This stuff will cut up your hands. Let me move this layer." And, with that, he quickly grabbed the edge.

As soon as he lifted it, a small dog bolted out from underneath, where she'd been pinned and unable to get free. "Pocket!"

Pocket raced to Brittany, jumping all over her in joy. Brittany laughed as she scooped up the little dog and held her close.

"Well, aren't you a sight for sore eyes," she cried out in joy.

The stranger put the tin roofing on the ground and smiled at her. "A happy dog."

"As she should be." Brittany rubbed her all over. "Especially considering that she's been under there for days. I've been looking for her all this time. Only today did I hear her yelp."

"She might not have heard you with the noise around here," he suggested, "and maybe she's been unconscious too."

"I'll get her to a vet and checked over," she said. "Thanks for the assist. Where are you heading? I am so sorry. ... I don't even know your name."

"I'm Baron," he replied, with a grin. "Brad was a good ten years older than me." Her eyebrows shot up, and he nodded. "I was a latecomer, ... which has been an ongoing joke in the family. My mother tells me that I was still welcomed though."

At that, Brittany smiled. "I'm Brittany, and I'm guessing she was pretty happy to have you, regardless of when you showed up."

"Isn't that the truth?" He reached down and stroked the little dog's head. "She really is pocket-size, isn't she? She'll be hungry, but, as soaked as everything is, she might have had sufficient water under there." He turned to look back at the roofing he had moved. "She was pinned pretty tightly under that though, so she's probably a bit dehydrated. She'll need some food but only a little at a time at first."

"I've got food and water in the car," she noted.

"Have you seen any other dogs around here?" he asked, turning to survey his surroundings.

"I thought I did the first day, but it's been such a mess. I'm not sure that I would say it was a dog versus something else, like a coyote," she murmured. "So, I really don't know."

"Where did you see it?" he asked.

She pointed down several blocks. "It wasn't terribly friendly, so I wasn't sure and didn't get that good of a look. We were all making so much noise too," she added. "Then, every time a vehicle comes up, people generally hide, you know, in case it's the authorities trying to kick us out because it's not safe and all. Most of the people are the neighbors who lived here. We've been trying to sort out if anything is left to salvage."

"Yeah, I came here for that too," he shared, sorrow in his tone. "My brother's place is just a few blocks over and yet was almost completely missed by this. There's a little damage but not much."

She nodded. "Good thing it did. You've already lost your brother, so you didn't need to lose all his things too." At that, the little toy poodle in her arms licked her chin and wiggled rather frantically.

"You should go feed her," he said, with a smile. "She's

looking a little on the desperate side."

She put the little dog on the ground, and the dog ran around in circles, yelping. "I need to get her back to my grandmother too," she noted. "That would make her day more than anything."

"Unless she has to go into a home and then can't take the dog with her."

She winced at that. "I hadn't considered that. Good Lord," she muttered, looking back at the house. "It's killing me to see it like this. Nothing salvageable is here."

"Get Pocket checked out, and I'll keep looking."

"Looking for what? You never did say," she asked curiously. "What are you looking for?"

"Sorry, I guess I didn't. When Brad's truck was found, some of the rescue dogs were still in the back, but others were missing. It's not as if we have any records at this point. Everything happens so fast in these storms and in the aftermath. People just do the best they can and hope for the best, but it doesn't always happen."

"Oh." She winced. "I didn't even think of that. So, he never got to finish the trip?"

"No, he didn't, and I want to ensure that any of the animals he was out here risking his life for are saved."

She nodded, looking up at him, realizing how fresh the loss was and just how much this mattered to him. "I'm so sorry. ... It's one thing to lose possessions, but it's another thing entirely to lose a family member. I know you said it wasn't because of this event, yet at the same time it was."

He nodded. "Exactly, and that's the discussion I'm having with my mother right now. A part of her really hates everything to do with this work, and, at times, she blames the hurricane."

"And yet it wasn't the hurricane."

"Exactly," he agreed, with a smile. "If it wasn't the hurricane, then chances are it would have happened anytime. Yet, without the stress of the hurricane, she thinks he might have lived longer."

"Oh, that's a rough one too," she muttered, staring at him. "I hope you find a way to make peace with it."

"Well, if I could find the dogs he was working so hard to rescue," he noted, "it would at least bring me some closure."

She nodded. "I don't know anything about which shelters he was working with out here. I did see him earlier at one point, when I was trying to get my grandmother out, and she wasn't being very cooperative," she shared, with a sigh, "and he did have a truckload then."

"A truckload of what?" he asked her.

She frowned as she thought about it, dragging her mind back to the last time she had seen Brad. "I saw the cages with dogs in them, but I don't know which dogs." She raised both hands. "He had a lot of them."

"Large, small?"

"Yes, all kinds. There did appear to be shepherds in there, but more than a few people around here have shepherds."

"Well, the one I'm looking for," he began, "was a War Dog, with somebody scheduled to look after him, but then, when the hurricane hit, I guess they left the dog behind."

She stared at him in shock. "That's not fair. Poor dogs."

"Yet you know it happens on a regular basis. So what are they supposed to do, when they have minutes, or seconds, to get out or into a shelter of some kind."

She winced and nodded. "You're right. I saw that here myself," she muttered, "and I can't judge other people for it.

Sometimes they have literally seconds to run, and, in the face of that monster hurricane, no doubt it's every man for himself," she noted. "But if Brad had the War Dog in the truck, you would think it would have been there with the others."

"His cage was empty, per reports I'm getting, and I'm not even sure how long he has been out here," he pointed out. "If the dog got loose from the crate, he might be out here helping somebody else or foraging for himself."

"Oh, I really like the idea of him out here helping," she replied, "particularly if it's a dog trained for search and rescue or something, though I don't know how that all works."

Baron nodded. "A ton of variables are involved. And just as a lot of soldiers came back in various conditions, the War Dogs did too. So, I can't make any assumptions about this particular War Dog, not without talking to someone who has handled him recently. I would love to think that was an option, but I need to find a way to confirm it. It would be great to talk to the dog sitter, or, who knows, maybe I could get more from the War Department."

"Maybe you should give it a try," she suggested. "Seems to be a good way to move forward to me."

He grinned at her. "That's because you want a happy ending."

"I need a happy ending on something around here," she stated, as she stared around at the mess. "We all do."

His smile faded away, as he looked at her. "You're right. I'm sorry, I didn't mean to make light of it."

She shook her head. "And I didn't mean to make you feel bad. Honestly this has all been such a challenge that it's hard to know what any of us are supposed to do at this point."

"We each do what we always do," he said. "We survive and do the best we can, one day at a time. It's bound to be a situation of just putting one foot in front of the other for a long time, but it will get better."

"Got it." She chuckled. "Glad it's that easy."

"It's not that easy," he countered, shaking his head. "It's not easy at all, but it's doable, and it's the only real way going forward. So that's what we have to hang on to." And, with that, he lifted a hand, "If you hear anything or see anything …"

She frowned. "I need your number. I can't contact you without that."

He brought out his phone, and they quickly exchanged numbers. "I'll text you, if I see anything."

She nodded. "That would be a relief. Lots of people here are still missing their pets. I'm so glad to have found Pocket, and I really appreciate your help. I could have never gotten her out by myself. Not many people are lucky like that. I know for sure the neighbor here has two Labs, and they haven't found them either, so if you see them …"

"Will do," he replied. "I'll keep you posted. Maybe we should have a database or something."

"I know the search and rescue people had one of the animal groups come in, and they were trying to pick up all the animals that had been left behind," she shared. "I don't know if maybe the Labs are there. I did tell the neighbor to contact them, but I don't know if he has or not. I can't imagine anybody's had a chance to set up a database yet," she added, "so things were definitely uncoordinated and a mess."

"It often happens with natural disasters," he agreed, with a careless wave. "Yet it will improve and get better as they go ahead."

"I'm glad to hear that." She stared around at the house. "I just don't know what improvement I can even look forward to at this point."

"Did you live here with your grandmother too?"

She shook her head. "I'm over a few streets, but I'm in the opposite direction." She pointed to the north.

"Where's your grandmother staying now?"

"She's staying with a friend of hers at the moment, but it's looking as if my house is the next stop," she said ruefully. "That's something she may not be ready for, but, as they say, desperate times or whatever." She stepped back to give him room to leave. "Disasters or other unexpected events sometimes mean we don't have any choice, so we do what needs to be done, even if it wasn't in our plans." She waved at him as he left. "Let me know if you find anything."

"Will do. If you see or hear anything," he repeated, as he looked down at little Pocket, who was circling Brittany's feet, "let me know." And with that, he got into his truck and drove forward around the tree he'd so easily cut through.

She watched him for a long moment, until he disappeared from view, then bent down, scooping up Pocket. "That's really sad news about Brad," she murmured. "Yet Baron seems like a very interesting person."

Pocket just snuggled in close, not really caring what she said, as long as it was in that tone of voice that said she was safe after all her trauma. And, for that, Brittany was definitely in agreement. There were times to worry, and there were times when it was so much easier to just know that you were okay. Right now, that's all Pocket needed to know.

She carried her to her car, left parked a way down the road. "Let's go see Grandma."

With that, she got in the car with Pocket and left.

CHAPTER 2

B RITTANY SAT ACROSS from her grandmother, who was still cooing over Pocket, now safely nestled in her arms.

She looked up with tears in her eyes. "Thank you, dear. Thank you for finding her."

"Of course." She waited a few more minutes, as things calmed down, and she asked, "Grandma, did you know that Brad died?"

She looked over at her granddaughter, nodding. "I did hear something about that," she muttered. "He had a heart attack or something in one of the trucks, while he was rescuing dogs or something."

Brittany nodded slowly. "I didn't know."

Her grandmother frowned at her. "Does that matter?"

She shook her head. "I guess not, but I met his brother today."

"Oh, that would be Baron," she murmured. "I haven't seen him in quite a while. He was off in the military for a long time, but I heard he got hurt. What was he up to?"

"Apparently his brother *was* helping to rescue a bunch of dogs, and, when Brad had a heart attack, some of the dogs managed to get free. Others were still there in cages in the truck, until they were discovered and rescued. Baron is looking for the dogs lost from the back of his brother's truck."

Her grandmother beamed. "That sounds like those boys," she said, "very much animal lovers, and the people to have in your corner when you have a problem." She eyed her granddaughter closely. "So, what has you bothered about it?"

"I'm not sure anything bothers me about it," she replied, frowning at her grandmother.

Her grandmother nodded slowly. "They are good people. I've never had a problem with any of them."

"That's good to know," she murmured. "I just wondered about the dogs that he's going after."

"Meaning he shouldn't go?" she asked her granddaughter.

"Absolutely he should go, as long as it's safe," she clarified. "I just don't want his mother to lose another son."

"I think the hurricane danger is more or less over at this point. It's just the rubble and debris, which I'm not minimizing at all," she murmured, "but Baron is very sensible and, like Brad, an experienced rescue worker."

Brittany nodded but didn't have a whole lot more to say about it.

"What's got you in such a dither over it?"

She laughed at the old phrasing. "Nothing. ... Just interesting meeting him, that's all."

"Ah, he's probably the most interesting man you've met in a while, *huh*?" Grandma asked shrewdly.

Brittany flushed at that. Her grandmother was never one to miss an opportunity to point out Brittany's single state. "I'm just fine, thanks," she replied.

"Well, you might be fine, but it's a lonely world out there, and you could sure use some friends."

"I'm not saying I couldn't use some friends. I'm just saying that I don't need to be reminded all the time that I'm single."

"No, reminding you won't change it," Grandma conceded. "That'll take *you* stepping out of your little privacy box to do something about it."

She groaned. "We're not having this conversation right now."

"Nope, no need to." Grandma rose and headed for the dog treats for the umpteenth time.

"I really don't think Pocket needs more treats, Grandma," she pointed out to her grandmother. "She needs real food."

"She's had real food, and now she's had cuddles. So she can surely have a couple more treats," she replied crossly. "She went through a harrowing ordeal," her grandmother chastised Brittany. "Everybody should be allowed to have a few extra treats, when they've been put through such a thing."

Not a whole lot Brittany could say to that, and no doubt that Pocket had definitely been through a harrowing ordeal. Brittany just didn't think that dozens of treats would be very good for her. "You might want to remember," she added, "that her digestive system can't handle too much of anything right now. She didn't have food for all that time she was stuck under that roofing, so go easy."

Her grandmother sighed and put the treats back. "You're right. As much as I want to completely spoil her rotten right now, I don't want to make her sick."

With relief, Brittany smiled as her grandmother sat back down again and just cuddled Pocket. "I'm just glad she survived it," she murmured.

"I'm so glad you were able to find her," Grandma noted, with a smile.

"Honestly, Baron lifted all the heavy items off of Pocket, so that we could free her." She chuckled. "He did it quite easily too."

"A big strong, healthy man," her grandmother announced, "is very good to have around."

Brittany rolled her eyes. "But that's not the reason we have them around."

"Why not?" her grandmother asked, a twinkle in her eyes. "They're certainly helpful at times."

"Sure, but we don't have them around just so we can take advantage of their muscles," she argued, with mischief in her tone.

"There are a bunch of other reasons to have them around too," Grandma added, "but, if you're not ready for that, no point in discussing them."

She groaned. "I'm definitely not ready for that."

"Too bad, because there are definitely men I would recommend."

"Of course you would." Brittany groaned. "Thankfully I'm not in the market. So, when you do rave on and on about them, remember that."

"You're never in the market. You haven't been in the market since you got ditched at the altar." Brittany swore at that, and her grandmother winced. "I know. I know. I'm not supposed to bring it up, but surely it's old news by now."

"It might be old news, but that still doesn't mean it's anything I want to discuss."

"You've never wanted to discuss it, and you've never let it go. That's why it's never gone away," Grandma declared, studying her granddaughter.

"Enough," she muttered. "This is the last thing that needs to be discussed right now."

"Maybe not, I'll give you that. Maybe we should just all ignore the fact that you've let your entire life come to a standstill because of it."

Brittany wiped her brow. Her grandmother usually didn't go in this direction, so something about the hurricane must be getting her tongue to fly off the handle a little more than normal. Her grandmother wasn't easily appeased either. She appeared to be on a run and wouldn't let anything stop her right now.

"I've told you before," Grandma muttered. "You need to let that crap go and find yourself someone else."

"I would if I found anybody," she pointed out, "but, so far, I've not exactly seen anything I'm interested in."

"Not true," she argued. "You met Baron today. That's a good first step forward."

"Right, I just met him *today*," she emphasized, "so I won't jump his bones already."

Her grandmother stopped, an arrested look in her gaze, and then went off in peals of laughter. "I bet you could. I'm totally okay being here for a while if you want to meet up with Baron."

"Oh, good gosh," Brittany muttered, wishing she'd never brought it up.

"And you would enjoy it, you know,"

"Enjoying it is one thing," she conceded, "but I'm much more into relationships that are for the long haul. Anyway, enough of that. I really don't want to sit here and discuss this, if you don't mind."

"Spoil sport," her grandmother grumbled, as she turned her attention back to Pocket. "Just so you know, if he's out there rescuing other dogs, he might need a hand."

"I'm sure he has a whole team to back him up," she

pointed out. "The last thing he needs is somebody like me."

"Oh, I don't believe that for a moment," Grandma countered. "However, as long as you choose to, it will keep you in your nice little hole for that much longer." Then she got up, leaving no chance to respond to that insulting retort. "I'll go lie down for a while. Now that I have Pocket back, I think I can probably sleep."

"You do that," Brittany murmured, frowning with worry as she watched her eighty-three-year-old grandmother make her way to the small bedroom of her friend's house.

Just then, Grandmother's friend Camille walked in from the living room and looked in the direction of her grandmother, as she headed to the guest bedroom. "How is she?" she whispered.

Brittany smiled. "In many ways, very much the same as always and, in other ways, tired, old, sore, and devastated," she murmured.

"Of course," Camille muttered. "She's welcome to stay here for a while longer. You know that, right?"

"Thank you. I'm trying to figure out just what the options are."

"You know what the options are," Camille stated. "You just haven't reconciled yourself to them."

"I know … It's just not something I wanted to do right now."

Camille nodded. "I get that, but we don't always get a choice in these matters. Therefore, it might be time for you to suck it up and to accept that your grandma needs your help for a little bit longer and then just do it."

"Yet that little bit longer could easily be another ten years or more, and I don't exactly have the life that's conducive to caring for her."

"You work from home," Camille pointed out, "so it's not as if you won't be there. Plus you get along famously. The two of you are great for each other. So why would it not be conducive?"

"Because she likes her friendships, her bowling nights, her bingo nights," she replied in frustration.

Camille nodded. "Yet you know that I'll continue to pick her up and to take her with me to these events."

Brittany grimaced. "Thank you for that. She's very active—and I'm not. I don't particularly want to have her bridge club over on her designated week. I would have to clean house and have snacks. I like my peace, thank you very much."

At that, Camille grinned. "Hang on a minute. Does that mean you're jealous of her social life?"

Brittany groaned. "I'm glad you're having fun at my expense, but it isn't an easy decision to become a caregiver or to even look for one, much less to convince Grandma that she needs one."

"No, it isn't," Camille agreed, "and, as long as your grandmother had her house, it was a decision that didn't have to be made. But now, a decision must be made." Looking back toward the bedroom, she sighed. "I brought up her moving in permanently with me, but she abruptly waved me off, refused to discuss it. So, yes, this decision is not an easy one, I agree. Yet you must at least discuss it, and I would say sooner rather than later would be best. However, you don't really have any *sooner or later* about it. You are looking at *right now*."

Brittany nodded glumly, as she stared at the wall. "It's not that I don't love her, but it's such a huge responsibility to have her living with me."

"It *is* a huge responsibility," Camilla confirmed, "and I presume your mother is not around, correct?"

"No, my parents have been gone quite a few years now," she replied.

"And that was her only child, her only daughter?"

Brittany nodded again, knowing exactly where this was heading. "Yes, just the two of us are left." Camille didn't say anything to that answer, which was already enough to point out that, when the chips are down, really only family was there—and sometimes family wasn't. "The other issue is that she won't necessarily agree to come to my place," Brittany pointed out. "That is likely to be the biggest thing. I'm sure she'll need some convincing."

"Your grandmother is stubborn."

"Very stubborn," Brittany agreed, with a smile, "and very independent."

"And nothing wrong with that either."

"No, of course not, unless it's something that we want her to do, and she doesn't want to do it."

Camille chuckled. "Well, let's just take it one day at a time and see what she comes up with for an answer herself."

"That's what I've been hoping for, you know? That she would work her way around to the discussion and see what we have for options," she murmured. "I know what some of the options are, but I also know that they won't be options that she's particularly fond of."

"Exactly, but that doesn't mean there aren't other options available though."

But really it did mean that because, without tons of money, not a whole lot of other options were available to those on a limited income. Her grandma had her pension, but her paid-for house was her biggest asset. Now that was gone. And Brittany had no high hopes that the insurance company would pay Grandma anything near the true replacement value of the home. And did her homeowners insurance cover temporary housing costs? That would help. Brittany pondered all this as she got up and made herself a sandwich in Camille's kitchen and prepared one for her grandmother to eat when she got up again. Brittany would have to restock Camille's fridge, as the previous groceries were dwindling down. It was the least Brittany could do for Camille, while housing her grandma.

She asked Camille if she would like one, but, as always, she shook her head. "No, I'm fine. I've already eaten."

Brittany wasn't sure Camille had eaten anything, but it seemed to be an ongoing trend here between the older ladies, where they didn't eat hardly a bite. Deciding that was something else that needed to be broached, Brittany took her sandwich and sat back down beside her. "Okay, what's the deal? Why are you really not eating? Are you broke or is this something else I need to be concerned about?"

Camille smiled at her. "Are you telling me that you don't already have enough to worry about?"

"I have lots to worry about," she shared, "but having more to worry about doesn't mean that I'll worry any less."

Camille looked at her in confusion, then laughed. "That may have made sense to you, but it really didn't make any sense to me at all."

"I know, and that's okay too, but I do need to know that you're okay."

"I'm fine," she murmured. "I was thinking maybe I needed to take in a boarder or somebody, if not your grandma, but I'll probably be okay regardless."

"Moneywise, you mean?"

Camille nodded. "When you set aside a certain amount of money for your retirement, but inflation continues to go up along with the prices of everything, it can get scary. You think you have enough, but, all of a sudden, it goes to shit, and you don't have enough."

"Of course," Brittany murmured, "and I'm sorry if you've come to that point." She pondered it for a moment. "What if I could convince my grandmother to stay here with you? It would be one solution for both problems. That is, if you don't mind my sharing with Grandma how you could use the help financially."

She looked at her, then shrugged. "I don't think she would, but it's certainly something we could discuss." Camille frowned. "But I couldn't handle all your grandma's needs."

"No, you wouldn't have to," Brittany pointed out. "It would be something that we could split, which would give me a bit of a break. That way I could work and check in on a day-to-day basis. Maybe I should check out having a nurse drop in once a week or something. Even get you a maid to help with the housecleaning. I'll see how much each would charge, and I'll let you know more about it. Even though I know it's not affordable in Grandma's case, I may check into the assisted living places nearby and just see what that figure looks like. It would at least give me an idea of what the bigger picture entails, and other options."

Camille brightened a bit and looked intrigued by her ideas. "Maybe," she added hesitantly, "but I'm really not sure your grandma would go for it."

"No, she might not, but, at the moment, I don't think she'll go for any of the options we have."

Brittany left it at that, but she pondered it as the day

went on. After her grandma's nap was over, Brittany had taken Pocket and her grandmother to the vet and then back again. After spending the bulk of the day with her grandmother, she said goodbye and headed to her car. She remembered getting a text that she hadn't had a chance to even look at. She pulled out her cell and noted it came from Baron.

Surprised, she was a little bit confused as she read it. She wasn't sure exactly what he was asking, something about knowing the Gorman family and also the Galloway gang, but the text had been worded cryptically. Not sure what to think, Brittany quickly picked up the phone and called him. When he answered right away, she began, "Sorry, I got your text, but I didn't quite understand what you were asking. I felt like I'd come in the middle of a conversation."

"That's because I meant to send that message to someone else. Sorry."

"Oh," she replied, deflated.

"But, while I've got you, do you happen to know anyone from that family?"

"The Gormans? No, not personally. I've seen an old man around from time to time but come to think of it, I don't think I've seen him or anyone in a few years. Why?"

"People are living in their house, but I'm not sure whether it's them or possibly squatters."

"Well, it probably is. Not too many people are out that way right now, what with the hurricane and the debris and such."

"Right, and that's another reason why I'm questioning it. I don't know what you've seen for looters, but a few are around here."

"There are. I know," she confirmed, a bitter taste in her

mouth. "I was planning on coming back out there again, but, by the time I got Pocket to the vet, got Grandma calmed back down and ready for a nap and all the rest, the day got away from me."

"Of course it did," he agreed, with a cheerful tone.

"Did you have any luck finding the War Dog?"

"No, I haven't, but I won't stop looking for a while yet."

"Isn't it too late to even see what you're doing?"

"No, it's still pretty light out," he replied.

"Well, in that case, maybe I'll come back down," she suggested. "I'm just sitting in my vehicle outside my grandma's friend's house."

"I'll come over if you're alone. At this hour it can be much harder to find people."

She hesitated, then stated, "But sunset isn't for another good hour yet, so I should come down and do some more sorting."

"What exactly are you sorting?"

"Just sifting through her stuff for anything worth keeping," she muttered. "Grandma's pretty devastated to think she has lost everything."

"Ah, so you are hoping to find family mementoes and such things?"

"Yes, but you don't sound too impressed."

"I don't have much of that stuff in my world," he shared, "so it doesn't make a whole lot of sense to me, but I get it. It's important to other people, particularly to older people. Ma has our family photos and such."

"Exactly," she agreed.

"I bet your grandma was happy you found Pocket."

"She's absolutely ecstatic." She chuckled. "It sure made my day."

"Good. So why don't you just get some rest and come back out tomorrow?"

"Will you be out there tomorrow?" she asked hesitantly.

"I'll be out here tomorrow and the day after and the day after that," he noted. "I'm pretty serious about making sure that whoever is out here is okay and that, if the War Dog is still around, I find her."

"It's a her?"

"Her. Him. … I'm not even sure at this point," he admitted. "I'll have to check my files."

"How will you even know if it's her if you do find one? Other shepherds are around here too."

"There should be a tattoo," he shared, "and some other identifying marks."

"Okay, … as long as you're confident you can find the right dog."

"I'm pretty sure I can do that," he said, with a laugh.

"I guess I'll have to see for myself. Maybe I'll come down today, but maybe I won't."

"If you do come down, let me know," he suggested. "I don't want to think of you down here alone, not when the damage is so devastating. Remember that the rest of your grandma's house may fall down soon as well."

"Trust me that I know how it is down there," she replied. "I've been at her place every day since."

"Right. Well, you decide." And, with that, he hung up.

Hanging up made her decide. She quickly pulled back onto the road and headed the few blocks down to the wreckage of her grandmother's house.

She got out and stood here, looking at the devastation, wondering once again if there was any point in even trying to sort through this mess. They hadn't even had a call back from the insurance company yet. All she could do at this point was hope that her grandmother had paid all her premiums and didn't give the insurance company any room to wiggle out of covering this.

She knew that getting covered after this would be a problem as well. She already heard that sometimes continuing coverage was a problem, once a natural disaster had ripped through an area. Insurance companies didn't like it when you made claims to begin with, and they especially didn't like it when you lived in an area prone to having issues. But that was a problem for another day.

She sighed as she turned to look around, choosing for a moment to face the water, choosing to avoid the view of the trashed house while she could.

"Mother Nature, you can sure be a bitch sometimes," she murmured, as she stared out at the wrongness of the world around her. Such a beautiful shoreline and beach had been here, and now it was full of devastation, littered with broken boats, roofs, trash, and trees. What a mess.

It was just so upsetting to consider how much pain the storm had put everybody through, but they'd all survived to live another day. Then she winced, remembering that wasn't true. In fact, some of them, like Brad, hadn't survived at all.

She couldn't imagine what that would feel like right now. It had been tough enough on her grandmother, thinking that she had lost Pocket, but here Baron had lost his brother. Brad was one of the few really good people she knew in the world. He was always there with a helping hand and a big smile.

She recalled hearing something about Brad marrying for a short while many years ago. He didn't talk about it, even with nosy people asking too many questions, and she could understand that too. She'd spent way too much time trying to tell people to leave her alone too.

Sometimes they did, and sometimes they didn't. Curiosity got the best of everyone sometimes, and they couldn't leave well enough alone. In reality, Brittany was more than ready to step into a relationship, something she didn't dare share with her grandmother. Yet she had met nobody out there who was interesting enough to make her want to go in that direction again.

Except … she had to admit that Baron had caught her attention. He was definitely interesting, but he had his own issues right now. Yet, even with everything he had going on in his own life, he was still out there helping people. And animals.

That thought was unnerving, but she admired him for it. She wandered around outside her grandmother's place, picking up a photo album and a special cup that, surprisingly, was not broken. If a few familiar items like these would help make her grandmother feel settled and happy, it would be well worth the effort. Hearing a sound behind her, she turned to see Baron walking toward her.

"You were supposed to tell me if you came back down," he scolded.

She shrugged. "It was a random decision."

"You think a cup is worth it?" He pointed at the mug in her hand.

"Maybe not to me, but to my grandma? Yeah," she said. "It's not my things and memories that were lost. They were hers."

"Right," he said, with a nod. "It's always difficult to understand what's important to various people, and, for me, an old mug just doesn't cut it."

She held it up, smiled, and asked, "Are you kidding?"

He shook his head. "It's like one of those grandmother mugs, you know, probably somebody gave her three years ago."

She stopped, took a closer looked at it, then shook her head. "Actually I gave it to her, and it was at least ten years ago," she muttered, staring at it in amazement. "I barely even remember giving it to her."

"Well, apparently it mattered to her, if she kept it all these years."

"Wow," she muttered, "that is something I hadn't really considered." He looked at her curiously, and she shrugged. "Again it's not the stuff that we recognize as being important. It's all about what's important to them."

"I can understand that," he murmured, "and you found some photos?"

"I did, though it's getting too dark to really see very much," she noted, as she looked around. "Almost everybody else is gone."

"Exactly." He stopped and waited, almost as if he were expecting her to load up her finds and to head home.

She groaned. "I'm not used to being corralled into doing what other people want." When he looked at her with one brow raised, she shrugged. "You clearly are waiting for me to leave, but you can stand down."

"I don't know about the *stand down* part. Is that what it looks like?"

"Kind of, yeah." She chuckled. "It definitely has the look of you standing guard, wanting me to get safely on my way."

"Well, that is true," he conceded. "Absolutely I do, but I'm not really trying to force you into doing something you don't want to do. If you want to keep looking for something here, I can help."

"What about you?" she asked. "Aren't you leaving too?"

"Eventually. I'm not quite sure what I'm looking for at this point, but something is keeping me here." Surprised, she looked over at him, as he shrugged. "I know. Way too esoteric and weird."

"Maybe it's all about finding closure related to your brother."

He gave her a half smile. "Maybe. … It's a hard thing to determine when it's your family. You don't really understand, and you know that something major is gone, something which you can't ever get back. Yet you're still looking for the *why*. You're still looking for a reason that it happened."

"Ouch," she muttered. "That's rough, and I get it, but there are no *whys* in something like this and not any reasoning either. People get hurt all the time, and people die in these events. We do the best we can, but it doesn't mean that we can stop Mother Nature."

"I don't know about stopping her," he replied, "but I sure would like to turn back the clock. He … He was a good person."

CHAPTER 3

B ARON LOOKED OVER at Brittany and added, "Not to mention that I'm still looking for that War Dog."

"Which is also interesting." She stared at him with a puzzled expression. "Just that dog?"

"No, not just that dog, but I have been asked to look for that War Dog in particular."

"Ah, maybe that makes more sense, but a lot of dogs go missing in hurricanes."

"That's true. Tons of dogs go missing, but that doesn't mean they deserve to go missing." She frowned at him, and he burst out in a chuckle. "I don't mean to sound mysterious, but—"

"You're definitely sounding mysterious," she stated, "so something is still bothering you."

"Probably something here does bother me, especially considering my brother is gone," he admitted. "I'll deal with my current world, but it'll take a day or two."

"I understand," she said. "I've been trying hard to *not* invite my grandmother to come live with me, and I'm feeling pretty rough about that. Honestly I don't really want the responsibility, but I'm not sure how to make her life happen any other way."

"It is a huge responsibility," he pointed out.

"I know, which is a big part of my hesitation," she

murmured. "And I feel terrible for not jumping on it. What kind of a person am I? My grandmother goes through a terribly traumatic loss like this, and I'm not jumping up to saying, *Hey, come live with me*, you know?"

"Well, if I am not overstepping, … why haven't you?"

"I know I should—"

"I don't deal with the emotional side of it all. The military sucked all the joy out of all that for me. What's your real reason?"

"There are a lot of reasons, plus a lot of questions and need for options."

"One being that she may not even want to go to your place?"

At that, she laughed. "You're right there. And I haven't even talked to her about it. Yet I don't want my life to change. And this would be drastic." Brittany shook her head. "Yet the same could be said for Grandma. Thankfully she's over at Camille's in the interim."

"Camille? Camille Rogers?"

She looked at him. "Yes, do you know her?"

"Yeah, I sure do. She's been here a very long time."

"She has, and she's pretty fascinating in her own right, but I think she may also be struggling a little bit financially. Maybe, I'm not sure. She's been very welcoming and generous with my grandma, but every time I try to cook or make her something, she refuses it and insists that I eat, but she doesn't."

He frowned at her and asked, "So it could be financial distress. Could she also have a health issue?"

"She's not really talking, so I don't know, though she did acknowledge how expensive things have gotten," Brittany shared. "So many times these older people aren't exactly open. They are of that generation that you don't talk about money, politics, or religion. So they won't really share what their concerns are. I did bring up the idea that if she could look after my grandma, … or if my grandma could stay with her, I could pay her as the caregiver, even sharing some of the responsibilities."

"How old is Camille? Plus, if you don't know how her health is, do you think that is wise?"

"She's younger than Grandma. If they could come to an arrangement, it could end up being a shared thing between us, but we'll see." Brittany waved it off with her hand. "I have time yet to finalize things."

"Good, because sometimes these things come up, and a snap decision has to be made—or worse yet, the person is unwell and doesn't have much time left."

"Oh God," she murmured, "I would hate to think that my grandmother was that close already."

"How old is she?"

"She's eighty-three."

"So, she is old enough for that to be a concern," he noted. "You never know when something could happen."

Just the thought of losing her grandma was enough to make Brittany's heart seize, and she nodded. "I guess I know that intellectually, but she's also a tough old bird and could go another twenty years."

He smiled. "I would like to see that. Plus, if she's anything like Camille, she *is* a tough old bird. Gosh, Camille's got to be," he paused, frowning, then asked, "what? … Late seventies?"

"I would think so," she agreed. "I don't know how bad Camille's financial problem is, or if it's even a thing. It's not as if she was opening up to me about it or anything."

"No, but maybe we need to do more to push her to open up, so we can get a better idea of what the problem is."

She glanced over at him, and, with a crooked smile on her face, she asked, "*We?*"

He chuckled. "Sorry. My mother would say, *Give me an inch, and I'll take a yardstick.*"

"Oh, and I thought that was just men in general," she teased in a sharp tone.

He stared at her and blinked for a moment, before bursting out laughing. "That could be true."

"Could be?" She just grinned at him.

"By the way, I don't mean to be insulting."

"Neither do I," she pointed out, "but sometimes it just ends up being that way."

"Me too. I apologize. This is entirely not my deal. It's your deal."

"Still, any suggestions would be welcome."

"Are you sure?" he asked, giving her a look. "I don't want to butt my nose in where it's not needed."

"*Not needed* doesn't apply in this situation," she murmured, "since we have an awful lot going on right now. Any ideas would be appreciated."

"Speaking of right now," he said, "you should be going home and dealing with your own issues for a change."

"Really? Do I look as if I have that luxury?"

"No." He brushed a big chunk of dirt off her face. "However, it does look like you've had a rough day."

She reached up, checked her cheek, and chuckled. "I really am in rough shape, aren't I?"

"I don't know about that, but you look like you've had a rough day."

"*Rough life* is more like it," she pointed out.

"I'm sorry to hear that. So, tell me. Are you ill?" Then he shifted uneasily for a moment.

She frowned and asked him, "Did you hurt yourself?"

"No, just that my prosthetic is causing me some trouble. I've been on my feet too much." When she stared at him, he shrugged. "You're not the only one with health issues, or at least people with issues," he murmured. He pulled up his pant leg so she could see his prosthetic.

"I had no idea," she said, looking at it.

"Good." He smiled. "It's not exactly the first thing I want people to think of—or worse, the only thing."

"No, of course not, but I don't think anybody would think less of you for it."

He raised an eyebrow and asked innocently, "Seriously?"

She flushed. "Okay, so any decent person would not look at you differently."

"Maybe, but, in that case, an awful lot of people are in this world who don't look at things the same way as you do."

"I understand," she muttered. "And I get some of that myself because my grandma's been on her own for quite a few years. I know she doesn't want to live with me, and, what's more, I don't really want her to. That's not all that easy to admit. Don't get me wrong. We love each other very much, but we'll probably kill each other if forced to live together." She gave a nervous laugh. "Yet now, … well, there may not be another option anymore."

"That's why you need to just rest and relax a little bit," he stated. "You don't have to make that decision right now. Give yourself a chance to sleep on it."

"It still feels like it's the only way though," she said, looking at him.

He smiled, then nodded. "I get that too, but I'm pretty

sure you'll find other issues in life you'll need to solve too. So maybe you can let this go for now and let some of that settle to the bottom. You need some time to process things, and, to do that, you need to relax."

She shook her head. "Wow. Do you say shit like that to strangers all day long?"

He burst out laughing. "Well, I try. I mean, I'm trying to be supportive."

"Yeah, well, … I'm not sure it's working out for you."

He shrugged. "Hey, at least I tried."

"You did, and now, since it's too dark to do much more out here, we're leaving," she declared, with a big grin on her face. As she walked over to her car, she added, "On the other hand, I could use some food. How about you?"

He nodded. "I was thinking I needed to figure out something for dinner. It's too late to go home and join my mother. She'll have eaten already. I texted her I wouldn't make it earlier. But now I'm getting hungry."

"Let's head down to the mainland. I know a joint that serves a mean burger, if you want to go get one together."

"I would like that," he said, nodding at her.

She flushed. "Yeah, I know. I don't usually do shit like this."

His grin flashed. "Well, I, for one, am delighted."

"Good," she said, "but, if you ever tell my grandma, I'll deny it forever."

At that, he burst into laughter. "So, what then? She's on your case over that too?"

"Yeah," she confirmed, rolling her eyes. "There are just some things that grandmothers apparently think you're supposed to do, and to have, and to be. Mine at least, anyway. And, right now, I seem to be failing her on all fronts."

"Not failing," he clarified, "just making her wait."

She grinned. "Definitely making her wait."

"Any particular reason?" he asked curiously.

"Yeah," she replied, not missing a beat. "The last guy I had a long-term serious relationship with left me at the altar," she muttered, "so I'm not planning on going down that pathway again."

He stopped, studied her with his all-knowing eyes, and asked, "Clive?"

She winced. "Oh *great*," she muttered. "You know him?"

"This is an old stomping ground for me," he shared, with a smile. "I'm sorry he did that," he murmured. "I heard something about it and couldn't believe he did it."

"Yeah, neither could I," she grumbled, "but it's not as if I had any choice in the matter."

"I don't know whether it makes you feel better or not, but I don't think Clive's any happier for it."

"I would like to say that I don't give a crap. And then I would like to say that I hope he's suffering," she added, scrubbing at her face. "Yet that's just not who I am," she declared calmly. "So I'll just leave it at that and hope he gets his shit together before he goes out and breaks somebody else's heart."

"I can get behind that," Baron noted, "and I think that's a pretty fair response."

"Too fair," she muttered. "I probably should be calling him out for being such an ass."

"You should," he agreed cheerfully, "but I don't think he's grown up a whole lot yet."

"No, he hasn't," she confirmed bitterly, "and that was the problem in the first place. I wanted to get hitched, but apparently he didn't. Yet he went along with it, until he couldn't go along with it anymore," she shared. "I just wish he'd mentioned it ahead of time. If he had just told me, I would have understood."

"Of course," he replied, "and that would have made your life a whole lot easier."

"A lot easier and a whole lot less painful," she added, suddenly emotional and red in the face. "Being stood up at the altar isn't fun."

He stared at her with a shocked expression and asked, "Like, stood up at the altar, for real?"

She nodded. "Yeah, after buying the dress, delivering the cake, the preacher in place. Yeah. The whole deal."

"Oh, crap. That must have been brutal. All your friends and families there, I suppose?"

"Yep. Hey, if you're going to be humiliated, you might as well do it at the maximum level."

He burst out laughing at that, to the point that she had to grin at him.

"I don't know what's so funny," she said, with a smile, "and I'm glad you're enjoying a laugh at my expense."

He immediately stopped. "Not at your expense at all," he corrected, his grin widening. "You have such a great attitude, despite Clive being such an idiot. I'm just loving the fact that you landed on your feet as well as you have."

"Well, my grandma thinks I should have been out crawling the town and already found somebody else by now," she explained, "but, since I haven't, according to her, I'm still dealing with it."

"*Nah.*" He waved his hands animatedly. "You're not still dealing. You just don't trust yourself."

She stopped in the act of opening the car door and

stared at him. He shrugged. "Can anyone blame me for that?" she asked.

"No, I am not saying that at all. You made a choice with Clive, and it turned out to be a bad one. So now you're afraid that, every time you look at someone, you'll just repeat the experience," he stated simply. "But you won't because you'll look at it from every angle, one million times over, before you put yourself in that situation again," he pointed out, with a big smile she thought was infectious. "So, trust in yourself a little more. I'm pretty sure you'll come out smelling like a rose."

She shook her head, just as another vehicle drove down the road, very slowly.

He watched it go by with a narrowed gaze. "Any idea who that is?"

She studied the vehicle and shook her head. "No, but it's come through here before," she muttered. "I sure hope it's not looters again."

He shot her a hard look. "That wouldn't be good."

"I know, but some of the people who have been out here are up to no good," she murmured, "and what we're looking at here is an awful lot of people looking for a chance to make some easy money."

"I'm not into anybody making money off other people's hardships," Baron declared, looking back to the vehicle. "Look. You go on ahead to the hamburger joint. I'll just check out what he's up to and get that license plate."

"Oh no you don't," she countered. "If you're heading off to do that, I'm coming with you." He stopped and stared at her. She nodded. "I get it. Not the response you expected, but that's just part and parcel of being in my world," she muttered. "So, guess what? I'm coming with you." He frowned, then opened his mouth to argue, and she cut him off. "Don't even bother. I've been trying to keep track of everybody who's been coming around here too," she shared, staring at the vehicle as it continued down the road. "I don't like anything about somebody coming at this hour of the night."

"And yet, if they think we're following them," he pointed out, "they'll just come back later."

"I know." She turned to face him and asked, "Suggestions?"

"You won't let me go find out on my own, will you?"

"Nope, I'm definitely not doing that," she stated.

He felt admiration for her stance but also a certain degree of frustration because she wouldn't pay any attention to what he preferred, though why should she? She didn't really know him either. He really wanted to head over to the burger joint with her, just to spend a few hours thinking about the good things in life. Yet, if these guys were up to no good, an awful lot of people had already suffered, and they sure didn't need any losers coming by and taking advantage of the hardship they were already in. "Let's take one vehicle then."

She smiled at him and then nodded. "That makes more sense. Let's take your truck, since it can handle the roads a whole lot better with all this storm debris."

Together they got into his vehicle. He turned on the engine and began, "Listen. If it gets dangerous—"

"Don't worry," she interrupted. "I don't have a death wish, but I also don't want to see everything people have worked for go up in smoke because of some asshole."

HE JUST SMILED and headed down the road after the vehicle. He hadn't gone too much farther when he shut off the headlights. She looked at him and whispered, "Why did you do that?"

"I don't want him to know we're coming up behind him."

She stared ahead. "We can hardly see the road."

"Your eyes will adjust in a minute. I can see quite a distance ahead," he shared.

"Fine," she muttered, "but it's not exactly comforting."

"No, but doing this stuff is never comforting."

"This stuff?" she repeated, slowly looking over at him. "Have you done *this stuff* before?"

He nodded. "I've done all kinds of *this stuff* before," he quipped, with a knowing smile. "That's what happens when you're in the military. You're called into different situations, including natural disasters. You're called into places to help out with whatever needs to be done and with all that comes with it. Lots of times I was on missions overseas. Sometimes on peacekeeping missions, sometimes active missions that weren't so peaceful," he shared in a casual tone. "But something like this guy?" he muttered, nodding ahead. "I have an odd feeling about him."

"I did too, both the first time and the second time." She opened her phone and added, "I'm not positive, but I think I have a picture of his license plate that I took the other day."

He handed her his phone and said, "Send that license plate number to a guy named Badger, will you?"

She hesitantly opened his phone and then asked, "You really think it's something we should keep an eye on?"

He looked at her and smiled. "Didn't you keep track of that license plate for a reason?"

"Well, yeah, but …" Then she laughed. "One of those things where you feel stupid because you did it, yet maybe it's a good thing I did."

"Of course it's a good thing you did," he stated, with a casual wave. "Just send it to Badger, and, if it's nothing, we'll hear back from him, and we'll know."

"Oh good." She had to get his pattern for the swiping of the phone to open it up, and, as soon as she did, she shared, "You have a couple messages here from him."

"Read them, would you?"

She quickly read them out loud, feeling a strange intimacy in doing so. "He's just looking for you to check in."

"That would be him."

"Is he the one, … the one you mentioned about the War Dog?"

"Yes, he's the one who specifically asked me to find the War Dog."

"Interesting," she murmured. "I never think of things like the War Department looking after retired War Dogs."

"I'm not sure that it's the department itself, as much as the job was handed to Badger and his wife, Kat, and they've taken to it very personally."

"That's good. I'm glad somebody out there cares enough to do it," she murmured.

"And that's why they've taken it on because they do care enough," he declared, glancing at her. "Nobody really wants to think about these animals out there suffering, after having given so much of their lives to the service."

"True," she murmured. She quickly copied over the license plate numbers and sent it. "I didn't send a message with it."

"That's okay. I'm pretty sure he's used to that," Baron

replied, with a smile.

"Were you in the military with him?"

"Not with him but with several mutual friends," he replied. "A lot of us came out less than 100 percent, and he's been helping a lot of us get on our feet and get back out there. Kat designed my prosthetic," he added, as he tapped his leg by way of acknowledgment.

"Oh, that's fascinating. I thought about doing something like that, but I didn't really have the smarts for it."

"What is it that you do?"

"I do a lot of data analysis," she murmured. "It's something I can do remotely, and I fell into it. It seems I have an affinity for it, so I've been working for the same company for a long time."

"So, it's a work-from-home job then?"

"Yeah, most of the time. They send me all kinds of reports. I sort through them and give them the bottom line. Sadly, most of the time, it's not happy news, but it's the truth. It's a valuable situation for me," she admitted. "They also hire me out to other companies at times, and I give them the bottom line at the end of the day. In some cases I go through stocks and different products that they have and point out which ones are doing better than others and why they should be streamlining their product lines," she shared animatedly.

"Sounds interesting."

"It's something that I would have thought people instinctively do, but they get emotionally attached to various products, so they keep them around, even though it's costing them. At some point in time nobody can afford the cost, so I'm like the sledgehammer, the final straw that says out loud what they already really knew was unavoidable." When he looked over at her, she shrugged. "I just fell into it. I have no idea what I would do if I ever got fired."

"Doesn't seem they can afford to fire you," he offered, with a smile. "Sounds to me as if you've got yourself a niche part of the world, and they're glad to have you. And you have the smarts to do anything you would want to do."

"Maybe so. I've been working for them for a long time, so we're generally on the same page when it comes to this stuff, and I make good money, so I'm happy there."

"Well, if you're living down here, you can't be doing too badly."

"And my place is paid for," she added. "I made that a priority years ago."

"Good for you," he murmured.

"But ..." she began.

"But what?" he asked.

"While I make good money for me, it's not enough for me and Grandma. And it's certainly not enough to put Grandma in a fancy retirement home where they would take good care of her no matter what. Plus, this might sound selfish, but I want to continue working. I like my life as it is. I don't want it to change. I guess freelancing and being my own boss and setting my own hours makes me set in stone, reluctant to change. Maybe I'm in that first stage of denial still." She turned to face him. "This is not how I saw myself living out the rest of my years."

Baron nodded. "I understand. Change is upsetting, even temporary ones. Big changes that are long-term are even worse. Just give yourself time to adjust, to take it in, to look at options. Thankfully you have Camille to take a little of that pressure off you in the interim."

Brittany sighed, seemingly calmer, then asked, "What

about you? Do you have your future planned out?"

"I'm good. I've got money from the military, not that anybody in the military makes great money," he noted, shaking his head, while keeping his gaze on the road. "No one does, unless you're higher up, one of the brass. Yet the thing is, I saved almost everything I made because everything was pretty well covered." He shrugged. "I did a lot of traveling on the military's nickel, and I saved as much as I could the rest of the time."

"I'm like that too," she said. "Not everybody is big on savings, but that's how I managed to get my place paid for early." She fell silent, as she realized that they were still continuing on in the sheer darkness. "So, do you have some special talent for seeing in the darkness?"

"I do, not that it's 100 percent foolproof."

"They would hear our vehicle though, wouldn't they?"

"They would, depending on where they are," he noted, "but the fact that we haven't seen them and that we've only got a couple houses left is interesting."

"Well, up there is one of those spooky houses," she muttered.

"You're talking about the Gorman place?"

"Yes, I am," she confirmed, with a laugh. "Now I know you're a local."

He chuckled. "It's one of those places where we used to scare each other when we were young," he murmured. "We used to come down to the beach and ride a bicycle around these blocks, but that was one of those houses we all stayed away from."

"Yeah, I always stayed away from it too. It's definitely the scariest house on the block."

"It was, for sure. I'm surprised it's still standing."

"Have you seen it yet? Is it badly damaged?"

"I've driven around since I've come back these last few days, but I haven't really spent too much time at this end of the street." He pulled off to the side of the road, and he called her attention to something, pointing discreetly. "People are moving around up there."

She peered through the windshield, and then turned to look at him, not really sure what she was looking at. "I can't see."

"In that case, you're staying here," he pointed out. "If you can't see what's going on, I don't want you in harm's way, much less any danger."

"What makes you think it's dangerous?" He gave her a lopsided grin that she was starting to recognize and could almost anticipate. "You think they're looters?" she asked.

He nodded. "I would say so. Let me go see what they have to say for themselves."

"You can't just walk up there and talk to them," she cried out.

"I didn't say I would, but we have to do something. Otherwise they'll strip this place clean."

"We could call the cops."

"Yeah, we could, but do you really want to bring them in, knowing that we're not supposed to be here either?"

She winced. "Right, I forgot about that part."

He chuckled. "Let me go talk to them, and we'll see."

"Letting you go talk to them sounds like a fool's mission."

He stared at her for a long moment. "So, what would you like to do?"

"I don't know." She looked around the place, squinting hard. "Part of me wants to turn around and run."

He nodded. "That's the smart part, but the hero part is the part that wants to do good in this world, and it's out there waiting to act in a way that will help protect things."

"They're just things," she pointed out.

"Do you think they're armed?" he asked her curiously.

She stared at him, her stomach starting to scream. "I would hope not," she whispered, "because now you've got me really worried, and I don't want you going out there."

"Is that because you don't want me to get hurt or because you're scared to be left alone?" he asked, and such curiosity filled his tone that she just looked at him for a moment, unable to say anything.

"I can't believe you're even asking that," she said. "Of course I'm worried about you."

He gave her the warmest smile that she had probably ever seen. "I do like to hear that." Then he opened the door, stepping out. "So, I say that, and then you go anyway?" she cried out.

"Well, somebody's got to do something," he said, "and I highly doubt that it'll go bad." But he didn't have the door opened for more than thirty seconds, when something slammed into his truck.

Hopping inside, he closed the door and pulled her down, so they were leaning under the dashboard.

"What the hell was that?" she whispered.

He looked over at her, his face grim. "Bullet."

CHAPTER 4

B RITTANY WAS STILL hunched underneath the dashboard when he turned on the engine, sat up a little bit, and started to back up. She couldn't understand how he could possibly drive in the dark as it was, but he was managing to. When he got his truck turned around, he headed down the road a little bit, and then he got out again.

She sat up, slipped out of the truck, and raced around to where he was looking at some trees. "What are you doing?" she asked.

He gave her a grin. "I'm blocking the road, so they can't get out."

She stared as he grabbed the chainsaw from the back of his truck, went over to a leaning tree, and proceeded to drop the tree across the road. She gasped and then stared at him. "That's freaking brilliant, but it's also stupid. They'll definitely know who did this."

"Yeah? Did you recognize my truck?"

"No," she admitted, "but that doesn't mean they won't."

"That's beside the point. What matters is, they'll have a lot more trouble trying to get out of here now," he said, "and, in the meantime, we'll contact the cops."

She held out his phone. "It's been buzzing like crazy."

He nodded, speaking into it. "Badger, what's up?"

"I could ask you that," Badger replied, his tone amused.

"Does this license number have anything to do with the dogs?"

"Well, I don't know about the War Dog," he admitted, with a chuckle, "but it does have to do with somebody looting the properties under lockdown after the hurricane."

"Where are you?"

"I'm here, along with Brittany, in my truck. The occupants of the vehicle whose license plate I sent you are rummaging through the neighborhood. I just dropped a tree on the road to stop them from taking off."

"Brittany?" Badger asked, his tone calm but curious.

Brittany leaned over and introduced herself. "Hey, my name is Brittany Terrace. My grandma's got a house here, and I live a few blocks away. Baron helped me find my grandma's dog earlier."

"I'm glad to hear that," Badger replied, a note of laughter in his tone, as Baron just rolled his eyes.

"It's all fine," Baron noted, a bit irritated. "I'm still looking for the War Dog."

"Oh, and I'm so glad to hear you're taking care of the War Dogs," Brittany added.

"So," Badger asked Brittany, "any sign of him?"

"Not specifically, no. I did know Brad, and I knew that he was helping a lot of the local dogs," she shared casually. "At one point in time, I saw him around here. He had quite a full pickup load, and he was talking to somebody."

Baron turned to look at her, his tone sharp. "Do you know who he was talking to?"

She stared at him and then shook her head. "I didn't recognize them, and they did look a little on the angry side, but then a lot of people here have been angry because we've been shut out of our homes. We've not been allowed to get back to our places, and most of us have things that we wanted to try and salvage, like whatever we can," she murmured.

"Of course," Badger agreed. "That's always a fight with a natural disaster. By the time you're allowed back in again, often not a whole lot is left."

"Well, in this case," Baron noted, "these suspicious guys are up at the Gorman place, and I'm not sure anything is left there."

In the distance, she heard a bark. At that, Baron stiffened and turned to stare into the darkness.

"Was that a bark?" Badger asked, his tone deep and sharp.

Baron asked, "Can you bring the cops down here quick for these two guys? I need Brittany to go home, and then I'm going …" He hesitated, looked at her and added with a chuckle, "I'm going hunting."

"Will do," Badger replied. "Go easy."

After Badger disconnected, she looked at Baron, and he knew what was coming next. "Hunting?" she asked pointedly.

He nodded. "It's what I do."

"Well, I'm really glad to hear that," she snapped, seething, "but do you want to clarify?"

That lopsided grin made her heart flutter, and he shook his head.

"You really don't want to know," he said, "and you won't like it."

"You'll go hunt them, won't you?"

He nodded slowly. "It's what I do."

"Is it what you did before you got injured," she asked, "or after?"

"BEFORE," HE REPLIED, shaking his head, "but the leg doesn't make a damn bit of difference."

He knew he sounded stiff, angry even, that she had brought up his injury, but it was to be expected. Most people expected him to be *less than* now, less effective, less capable, when in fact in many ways he found himself to be a whole lot better.

He certainly understood the value of life a whole lot more than he used to, and there were definitely other aspects to being injured and facing death multiple times. Even getting his legs back under him had been a life-changing experience.

"I'm not trying to insult you," she said, "but I don't want anything to happen to you. They've already shot at the vehicle—something I noticed you didn't mention to Badger."

He shrugged. "Didn't think of it, but I will."

"Will you?" she asked skeptically. "I hope he does get some law enforcement here."

"I do too," he agreed, "and soon because they'll be coming back this way fairly quickly."

"Then what are we supposed to do?" she asked, staring at him in shock. "It's not like we can just stand here and wait for them to blast through."

"I don't think they'll be blasting through anywhere," he noted, and he looked thoughtfully down the road. "Do you know if there are any other roads out of here?"

She shook her head. "I don't think there are, but I'm not seeing them coming this way either." She hesitated, and, as they both stared in the direction where the vehicle had gone, she pondered the situation. "Maybe they just haven't had a chance to pack up enough stuff yet."

"That could be it too," he agreed, with a gentle smile. "We'll give them just long enough to hang themselves."

She winced. "Do you have to use that phrase?"

"No, I sure don't," he said, his grin deepening, "but I like it."

She rolled her eyes. "I think you're bloodthirsty."

"No, I'm a realist," he clarified. "Now, I don't want anything to happen to you, so will you stay here, wait for the cops, go home, or what? It has to be your decision."

"What will you do?" she asked him suspiciously.

"Go down there and figure out which dog is barking nearby."

She frowned at that. "If I've learned anything in the time we have been together, … you're not going down there just after a dog, right?"

"No, not just a dog," he confirmed, "but it's probably a really good way to find out if it's the War Dog that I've been looking for." And, with that, he stared off in the direction from where the shot had been fired.

"I don't want to be alone," she whispered.

He nodded. "I don't want to take you with me because I don't want to put you in danger," he pointed out, then smiled at her. "The cops are right behind you." He tossed her the keys. "Take the truck back to your place. I'll meet you there in what, about an hour?" And, with that, not waiting to hear her response, he gave her the briefest of smiles and disappeared into the darkness, leaving her standing in shock.

CHAPTER 5

W HEN THE COPS pulled up, one of them came to her. "Hey, what's going on here?"

Baron had told Brittany to drive the truck back to her place, but, as she turned to face the cops, she realized no way in hell she was leaving at all. If Baron needed to escape, he would need his wheels. Of course, if he didn't know that his wheels would be here, that wouldn't help either.

She groaned, even as the cop gave her a gentle shake. "Are you okay? Are you all right, miss?"

She nodded. "I am, but we were shot at, and people are up ahead. We think they're stealing, taking advantage of the situation," she explained, waving her hands. "You know what it's like here."

Both cops nodded. "You need to go home now," the lead cop said, "and leave this to us."

She gave him a wry smile. "That would be possible, except that he's already gone up there to see what the trouble is."

"Who has?" the cop asked sharply.

She peered into the darkness to try and see who she was talking to, but it was almost impossible. The heaviness of the sky seemed to have filled every square inch of the world around her. The darkness had a blanketing effect all around them. "Baron," she replied. "His brother died up here the other day."

"Brad," the other cop replied, "she's talking about Brad."

"Yeah, and this is his brother, Baron."

"I know Baron," he said, as he turned to face the area where Baron had disappeared. "Did he have a weapon on him?"

"None that I know of," she replied. "Does it matter?"

"Well, these guys are likely to be armed to the teeth, since they shot at you already," he explained, "so I hate to see anybody up there with that kind of trouble."

"He didn't seem to be bothered though," she pointed out.

"No, he wouldn't be." He sighed, then turned to his partner and shrugged. "He's from special ops in the military. He's got a lot of those in-demand skills, from what I've known about him. If he's up there, I don't want to mess up his road show. Yet we can't have whoever's up there shooting at people."

"Or helping themselves to everybody else's stuff," she murmured. "I know that's pretty low on everybody's scale of importance right now, but, for a lot of these people, this is all they have."

"All that's left of your homes. I get it."

"Well, we're already dealing with very rough situations right now," she said, "and then to have these lowlifes coming in and stripping out the homes that have been left unprotected, that's hardly fair."

The cops nodded. "That's also why we tried to get everybody to leave the area," he pointed out, "including you."

"That's nice and all," she replied, "but it also just clears the way for the hoodlums who are here, taking what they want, not even bothering with a *please* and *thank you*."

He grinned at her spunk, his white teeth shining in the darkness.

She groaned. "I really am not in the mood for this." She glared back down the road where Baron had disappeared. "I wish he would come back."

"I am sure he will soon, but he won't come back until he's ready."

"Right, it seems you do know him."

"I know the family," he said, "and Baron was always the most stubborn of that lot. His brother was never quite so obnoxious in that way, just because of his heart condition."

"Everybody knew he had a heart condition, *huh*?" Brittany asked.

"Yes," he said, "at least the locals did." He looked over at his partner, who was already nodding. "Yeah, he had had multiple scares, and this end wasn't unexpected. However, just because you know something could happen, it doesn't mean that you're expecting it to happen. Still, in this case, … it did, and that's a huge loss to the community."

"Well, his brother is out there trying to prevent anybody from losing anything else," she muttered, as she stared at the truck. "He told me to take the truck and go to my place."

"Then you better go. We suggest you not leave the truck here because he won't be expecting it."

She turned and looked at him, "And yet …"

"No," he said, raising a hand, "if he told you to take the truck and go someplace, just take the truck and go there."

Her shoulders slumped. "And here I was thinking you guys might be on my side."

"We're not on anybody's side," he declared crossly, "except the side of right, which, in this instance, I'm sure can and will get a little bit confusing."

"Ya think?" she quipped, shaking her head. "It's pretty frustrating."

"But, if he expects you to take his truck someplace," he pointed out, "he'll expect it to be there, so he'll show up there. If he does, and you're not there, he'll come back into the danger area, looking for you."

She raised both hands in frustration. "Fine, I just wanted to wait here for him."

"Not happening," he said. "Either you're going out with us or you're going out ahead of us."

She stared at them. "What about him though? Surely you won't just leave him out there alone."

"That's not our intention," the other cop replied, staring over at his partner, "but you're the one who we have to watch out for."

"No," she snapped, "I'm not. This isn't a case of one or the other. If you're staying here, I want to stay here."

"No," the first cop repeated. "If Baron told you to move out, then you need to move out."

She glared at him but realized they wouldn't listen to her at all. "It's hardly fair that you guys are ganging up on me," she muttered. The one cop tried to hide his smile, but she caught sight of it anyway and glared at him. "What? Is this some macho thing?"

"No, it's some *keeping you safe* thing."

There was little she could do to argue with that, especially as they were nudging her toward the vehicle. "Fine, but, if something happens to him in there because you guys are out here arguing with me, it's on you."

"Which is another good reason for you to get moving," the lead cop said, losing his patience, "so that we can go help him."

"Fine," she muttered, then hopped into the truck, started it up, and backed out while they watched. As soon as she was heading in the right direction, they took off in the direction she had told them Baron went.

If nothing else, she'd cleared the way for Baron to get some assistance. She didn't know that he wanted any, thinking he seemed to be more of a lone ranger type, which wasn't a bad thing per se. But both policemen knew Baron and seemed to be clued in on that, so hopefully it would work out okay. It would be better if Baron knew exactly who and what he was dealing with, but she didn't think he had any clue. None of them did yet. Unless Badger was able to get some information based on the license plate number she had sent. She could only hope.

She headed back to her grandmother's house, thinking that's what Baron had been talking about in terms of her location. But when he had specifically mentioned *her place*, what did he mean? She wasn't sure, but he would need a ride somewhere along the line, right?

Feeling like she was going a little bit crazy by questioning everything she was doing, she checked the time. Baron had left twenty minutes ago. He did say to give him an hour.

She couldn't tell heads or tails from this point, and it was starting to wear on her. As soon as she pulled up in front of what was left of her grandmother's house, she hopped out and walked up to where the front door had been. Not really anything was left anymore. She could push around the debris, but what good would that do her grandmother, if she was literally sitting here with no place to go? Apparently Brittany now had some time to figure out her grandma's housing issue.

Creating a space for herself, Brittany plunked down into

the middle of what was left of her grandma's house and just waited for Baron to return. A weird dark serenity surrounded her that gave an edgy look to the night. Of course, the fact that people were out there, potentially chasing Baron down, even as she sat here, was also unnerving.

She didn't know that he even knew where her own house was, so it made more sense to wait here at her grandma's place, and she really wanted to ensure that Baron was okay. This was closer too, if he came back needing help. She didn't even want to question why she was so worried about him, but, as her memory bank dredged up all the times she had been around Brad and how he was, she realized there were a couple times when Baron had likely been with him.

She thought about trying to reach for those memories going back, since she'd gone to school here too. Baron could have been a few years ahead of her, and Brad had already graduated from high school back then. Baron had told her that he was ten years younger than Brad, so Baron had to be few years ahead of her in school. With that, she remembered his latecomer retort, and it brought a smile to her face.

Only as the time ticked by did it suddenly hit her. Baron had been on the football team and potentially the baseball team, one of those jocks who were loved by all, and yet … She frowned at the thought that came to mind.

He didn't look like a typical sports jock, who barely had the brains to carry on. Instead he looked like somebody who had made a lot of choices in life that were exactly what he'd wanted and had done something with it. For that, she was happy for him. Yet it was odd thinking of him being an athlete, and yet he remained fit, outside of that leg, and she wondered if that even made a difference.

When she heard an odd sound, she immediately stood

and wanted to call out, then froze because whoever was approaching wasn't calling out to her.

She moved back into the darkness a little deeper, hoping she would see something ahead of whoever was coming her way. Even as she watched, she could see somebody, some movement coming toward her in the darkness, yet it wasn't anything she was expecting. If that was Baron, he would have called out for her.

Frowning, she waited, hating the uncertainty, then suddenly he was right there in front of her. She gasped in shock, almost screamed, before he clapped a hand on her mouth.

"Sorry," Baron whispered, "I didn't mean to scare you."

She shook her head. "Good God," she muttered, "couldn't you have at least warned me?"

He winced. "I was trying not to let the people behind me know that I'm here."

She stared at him in shock, frantically searching the darkness. He pulled her deeper into the house, or at least what remained of the house. "We'll just wait here for a few minutes," he breathed against her ear.

She nodded but hung on to him tightly, and he let her. Absolutely no backing away. As a matter of fact, he pulled her deeper into the shadows and held her close. She breathed up against his ear, "Is there one or two?"

When he squeezed her twice, she took it to mean two. She stiffened, then pressed herself tighter against him, waiting to see what would come of this. She trusted him, but the last thing they needed was violence.

When he relaxed slightly, she glanced around but couldn't see any reason for the easing up of his tension.

When he finally dropped his arms, he leaned closer and whispered, "Looks like they're gone."

She shook her head. "How the hell can you tell that?"

"I'm listening to the wheels."

She strained her ears, but, with the winds picking up around them, it was hard for her to tell anything. She could smell the scent on his jacket, and she wasn't sure what it was exactly, but maybe from a dog. She frowned. "Did you find the dog?"

He shook his head. "No. Why?" He looked down at her curiously, and she shrugged, embarrassed to have asked. "What? Do I smell like it?" He was openly laughing at her now.

She gave him a sheepish look. "Your jacket does."

"Yeah, it's my brother's." He ran his hands down the front of it. "I didn't even think about that. I just grabbed it when I saw it. We used to have matching ones way back when," he shared, "and I figured I would like to have it."

"I think that's a great idea," she shared. "He would have loved for you to have it. I'm sure of it."

"Well, it might not be such a great idea if it smells like dog to the extent you can smell me coming."

"Not from a distance," she noted, a smile in her tone, struggling hard to not devolve into full-blown laughter. Just something about his sense of humor, and maybe just about being around him, was freeing somehow.

In the distance, she noted that the wind suddenly went still, and then she heard the low drone of a vehicle coming from afar. "Is that what you were talking about?"

HE NODDED. "YES,"

"Did you get a chance see who it was? There are cops

out there, and of course you downed that tree …"

"There was room to move around it slowly. And it wasn't cops." Baron shook his head. "However, I didn't see who it was, but I did get the make of the vehicle."

"We have the license plate from before."

"Yes, assuming that it was the same vehicle and that it was the real license plate. People up to no good sometimes switch plates."

"Ah, so knowing the make will help confirm that, if we get something back on it from … What was his name?"

"Badger. I'll check with him later to see if he came up with anything. It was good instincts to get that plate number."

"Maybe I need better instincts," she noted, "because I could have been collecting a lot more."

He shrugged. "Or maybe you could keep yourself out of circumstances like this, and then you wouldn't need to use your instincts all the time."

"I don't know. I seem to be pretty good at getting myself into trouble these days," she muttered. "Did you see the cops?" she asked, then looked back to the Gorman place. "Where are they?"

He frowned at her. "I didn't see any cops."

She stared at him in shock. "Two of them went out there to help you."

"Help?"

"Yeah, … well, I don't know what you call it. Just a few minutes after you left, two of them arrived, and they went in to see if you needed help. They wanted me to leave first, so they could go look for you, but they wouldn't leave me there. They only left to search for you after I took the vehicle out of there."

"That's smart," he said, but his tone was mild.

That gaze of his was anything but, as he stared into the distance. "Do you think they're in trouble?" Then she shook her head.

"Problems?" he asked.

"No, I'm just an idiot." He looked at her again, and she shrugged. "I shouldn't say things like that."

"We all say silly things at times," he noted. "As long as you're okay, let's get you back up to your house. Plus you need to check on your grandmother."

"No, I told her that I was heading down here earlier, and she was planning on spending a quiet evening with Pocket."

"Right, and Camille is there."

"Yes. I've been thinking a lot about that this evening too, wondering if I should just be signing up Camille to look after my grandma."

"You need to know more about Camille's health, and even your grandma's. You know how the older generation keeps secrets, especially if it'll impact their freedom or would impose on their families. Especially the women of any age, who think they are supposed to look after the rest of us. You must have a serious conversation with both of them. See what Camille wants. See what your grandma wants. That would be a big commitment for Camille as well. Plus their living together might damage their relationship too, as you feared it might damage your own relationship, when considering living with your grandma. Just think of your grandma giving up her independence to rely on her friend Camille or even you. Regardless I'm sure it would also be a struggle for you."

"I know." Brittany sighed. "Mother Nature blew in, and now this new problem has landed on my plate, and I'm still struggling with it."

"It's not 100 percent on your plate either," he pointed out. "You do have some time, not a whole lot, but you can consider other options."

"I can consider other options, but Grandma would want to live alone again. If forced to, she would live with me, rather than a retirement home or even with Camille. Grandma was more than happy to be living alone, until reality came crashing down and took away her home." Brittany pointed to the rubble around them.

"Of course, and you can understand that too."

She nodded. "I do. I'm just not sure I'm ready for that big of a life change."

"Sometimes we don't get an opportunity to get ready for anything. We just have to do what needs to be done." Not a whole lot she could say to that. He motioned at the truck. "Let's get you home."

She hopped up in the passenger seat, and he drove her to her car. Once in and heading back to her house he followed.

He watched as she parked then walked over to him, staring back and muttered, "It really feels wrong to leave Grandma's house with armed looters running amok."

Leaning out of the truck he looked back when she was looking. "Do you want to go back in?"

She looked at him and nodded. "I want to, yes. I'm just not sure it's a smart thing to do."

"It's definitely not a smart thing to do," he declared, looking at her calmly, "but, if you just wanted to crash in her house, we could."

"Crash on what?" She cut him off, looking at him as if he had lost his damn mind.

"Anything you want," he replied cheerfully. "How about

a piece of roofing?"

"Ouch, no, thank you very much. I would really like better sleep than that."

"I'll be back in the morning again and will look around." She looked up at him, he nodded. "I'll be looking for the War Dog."

"And yet … it's probably a long shot, right?"

"Maybe, but if it was that important to my brother, I would like very much to solve it for him."

She sighed. "He really was a nice guy."

"I'm really a nice guy too," he added, with a chuckle. "You just don't know me as well as you did him."

"I was thinking about that earlier. Were you on the football team?"

He looked at her and then nodded. "Yeah, I was, and a few other teams. I was pretty active in sports in high school. I was never really a jock, but I was always on the teams. I liked to play everything and probably could have gone to college on a scholarship, but I just wasn't interested."

"I'm sure that probably gave your family the shudders."

"Well, it gave other people's families the shudders, if I remember correctly. My dad wasn't particularly bothered, as he didn't see me as a pro … anything."

"Did he have trouble when you went into the military?"

"No, I don't think so. I think he thought it would make a man out of me," he shared, with a laugh.

"Did it?" She couldn't help asking.

He glanced at her and nodded. "I would have to say yes, though it's not the easiest way to get there."

"No, I don't imagine it is," she agreed, "but I'm sure he was proud of you throughout it all."

"Well, if he wasn't, there was no making him happy,

because we both stepped up all the time," he shared. "He was a heavy taskmaster type with us and not exactly an easy person to live with, but we were all the better for it."

"How is he now?"

"He passed on a few years ago and now? … Well, I'm happy that my dad and my brother are together."

"And yet …" She hesitated.

"And yet what?" he asked bluntly.

"Then answer the question because you keep making those half comments and then stopping." She winced. It was a bad habit that she'd picked up years ago. "It just feels as if you're very unsettled about your brother's death."

"Unsettled?" he repeated calmly.

"Just because you know that something *could* happen doesn't mean you're ready for it."

"We knew that he could die from this at some point in time, but it's not as if we had any prior warning that it would be last weekend," he shared. "So, am I unsettled? Yeah, I probably am, but I can't think of anything I could have done to have made it any easier on him."

"No, of course not," she agreed, "and you can't feel guilty about it either. You weren't here, and, with his condition, there wouldn't have been much anyone could do."

"No, but I was on my way. He should have waited for me," he stated in frustration, "but it's typical of him that he didn't."

"Would you have waited?"

"No, I wouldn't have either," he admitted, with a nod in her direction, "and I know that, but it doesn't make it any easier."

"Well, we can go somewhere else if you want. Besides,

we never did get those burgers." She sighed. "I haven't eaten." His eyebrow shot up, and she winced. "I am definitely a foodie," she muttered, as she glanced around. "I'll have to head out and get food. We were talking about going out for food before—"

"We were, and nothing's changed," he said. "Are you still up for it?"

"I am," she muttered, "particularly now."

"Why now?" he asked, amusement in his tone.

Flushed, she crossly replied, "Because I'm hungry, damn it, and I try hard never to go to bed without a meal in my stomach."

"Okay," he agreed agreeably, "I'm with you there, but … are you okay? Your reaction just then was kind of wild."

"I know," she muttered, raising her hands in her defense. "I had an eating thing when I was growing up. It took me a long time to get over the worst of it, especially after that whole *being left at the altar* thing."

"We all have our coping mechanisms."

"Yeah, we do. So, for me, I try hard not to forget about food. I try hard not to go to bed without having eaten at least something. So, when I realized how late it was—and that I hadn't eaten dinner—it just hit me hard." She laughed. "I probably sound like I'm three sheets to the wind."

"Which would be fine," he noted, "but you aren't, and we did get a little sidelined, so I don't think this will be a horrible change to your plans."

"I hope not," she added. "Let's go get food. I don't know about you, but I need to eat."

He laughed. "I could do with food. I was running

around out there in the dark," he pointed out agreeably, "so I burned through a few calories."

"Right," she noted. "That is something I try to avoid doing."

"What? Burning through calories?"

She winced again. "No, not burning through calories," she countered, with an innocent smile.

"What then?"

"Mentioning calories and trying to burn through anything," she said, now looking not one bit ashamed of it. "That goes along with the eating disorder thing. I used to count calories meticulously and then kept moving until I burned up enough calories according to all the charts, so I never had anything left to be hung around on my body."

"Oh, wow. I've never known anybody with an eating disorder background, so I really don't know that much about it."

"Yeah, well, you may not want to by the time you figure out who and what I am," she said, with a laugh. "It's pretty easy to mess yourself up."

"It also seems that you've done a good job on straightening yourself up," he noted, giving her a searching look, "so cut yourself some slack."

She glanced at him and nodded. "I keep trying to."

"Try harder."

She groaned. "You'll be one of those, won't you?"

"Nope, I won't be one of anything," he declared. "You obviously made a lot of changes. You know what you need to do, and you're doing it. So, instead of getting hung up on it, you can admire your progress instead. I'm really glad to see that you're not ashamed of it and just own it. It's not a bad thing."

She straightened up in the seat and looked at him with confusion, then smiled. "Most people have something completely different to say when they find out I had an eating disorder. They say the stupidest things. Anything from *Oh no* to *Of course you didn't* or, one I particularly hate, *It couldn't have been too bad. You're a great weight now.* The rest I just ignore as *blah, blah, blah* because that's exactly what it is."

He shook his head. "I would never do that because it's your eating disorder. It's your body, and I couldn't possibly have any idea what you went through." He eyed her intently. "So, not my cup of tea. I think sometimes people have no idea what to say, and then the dumbest things come out."

CHAPTER 6

A S SOON AS they pulled into the parking lot of the hamburger joint, Brittany hopped out. She waited for Baron to join her, and the two walked into the small café together. She knew that would cause some comments, but she really didn't give a crap right now. If people wanted to gossip about them, well, they could. She was too hungry, too tired, and too damn fed up to worry about it. She headed to her favorite table in the far back.

Baron nodded approvingly.

"Oh, wait, hang on a minute," she began. "Did I do something instinctively right?" He just grinned at her. "I did just do something, right?"

He kept grinning at her for a few moments. "Let's just say that, given the circumstances, I would have chosen the same place to sit."

Her eyebrows shot up, as she slid closer to the window, where she could look out. "Are we expecting trouble?" she asked in a whisper.

"No, I'm never expecting trouble, but that doesn't mean trouble isn't right around the corner." She frowned at him, and he just smiled. "And, no, I'm not the person who's always looking for trouble."

"No, maybe not," she conceded, "but I have a hunch it has a way of finding you." His mouth burst into a big grin at that, something she wanted to bring on more and more. "You should do that more often," she shared abruptly.

He stared at her. "Do what?"

She shrugged, realizing it would sound foolish. "Smile."

His grin grew bigger, spreading across his face. "I do tend to smile a lot, you know. It's just … I haven't had a whole lot to smile about lately."

She winced, feeling completely insensitive. "Once again, I forgot. I am sorry."

"Don't ever be sorry for being honest," he stated, shaking his head. "You're right. … I probably should smile more. Yet, after recovering from my accident and slowly getting back on my feet again, there has been less to smile about than usual."

"I went through something like that with my grandma. She's had one hell of a scare after another, and now with losing her house …" She stared gloomily out the window, her good mood instantly gone.

"The problem isn't your grandmother, you know," he pointed out. "The problem is you. You'll feel guilty if you don't bring her home, and yet you don't even know if that's what she wants."

She nodded. "I know that independence is big for her. I really do understand that. Giving up her car was a big deal, but at least she had me or Camille to drive her around. I wouldn't want to give up my car either. Now she may have to give up living alone. The thing is, I just don't know how she can have that again, given the state of her health and the damage to her property now."

"I really think you're putting too much on your plate right now," he suggested. "So let's figure out where this is all going in the short term, and then we'll know more."

She smiled at him and then at the waitress, who came over and handed out menus. Brittany already knew exactly what she wanted. "I'll get a double cheeseburger with a large order of fries and a milkshake," she ordered quickly.

The waitress wrote it down, then turned to look at Baron. He just dipped his head. "What she said."

The waitress grinned, grabbed the menus, and asked if they wanted coffee. He shook his head. "No thanks. I'm good."

She looked over at Brittany, "What about you, ma'am?"

She shook her head. "No, just the milkshake. We'll have that first, please."

The waitress gave her a look and then disappeared.

Baron turned his attention to Brittany. She was fiddling with her hair. "Sounds like you have a bit of history here too."

"Yeah," she replied, looking back to where the waitress headed. "She knew me when I wasn't eating, as the saying goes."

"She should be happy that you are eating now."

"She also knows that I slide at times," she admitted.

"When was the last time that happened?"

"Years ago, but, once you slide, everybody keeps a wary eye on you, as if you'll collapse."

"And did you collapse on her?"

She shook her head. "No, I was at a baseball game with some friends, and I hadn't eaten all day. Mind you, it wasn't deliberate, but I was forgetful," she noted, with a roll of her eyes. "Nobody let me forget after that."

"Of course not," he agreed, "but think of it this way, … at least they're looking out for you."

"That was the theory I was working on," she shared,

"but it was still hard because it felt to me that I had failed everybody all over again."

"You didn't fail anybody," he pointed out, "and definitely not yourself, so you can knock that theory right out the window."

She burst out laughing, smiling as she turned to him. "You're good for me."

"Yes, I am," he concurred, with that million-watt smile, and it was infectious. "Anything you need to do to make yourself feel good, you should do it. Everything else be damned."

"I do feel good, and I've come a hell of a long way," she declared. "I'm just very aware that my history here gives a bit of edginess to all my relationships because I always feel as if I'm under a microscope, with people always watching me."

"Well, you're eating, so she should be happy. That should be it."

She nodded. "You would think so, but I don't know. I'm probably just supersensitive."

He didn't say anything but just watched her.

When the milkshakes came, she gave him a big fat smile. "If you don't want yours, I'll drink it too."

He chuckled. "We'll see about that, but I haven't eaten all day either."

"Ooh, watch out," she teased. "If they find out you haven't eaten, they'll think you have an eating disorder."

He shook his head. "Not likely. In the military, you learn to eat when you can, and you ensure that you *do* eat because you don't know what's coming."

"That's got to be tough at times."

"You get used to it. After being injured, I found that I needed to keep up my strength at all times so I could get through rehab, going through all the exercises, then getting rest to rebuild muscles," he explained. "I focused on high protein and did my utmost to get the calories in that I needed. I was never hungry because I was always eating so much, and, if anything, people were saying that I ate too much and would get fat."

"I can't imagine you fat," she replied, as she studied him.

"Just as I can't imagine you on the edge of dying from an eating disorder."

"I don't know if it was that bad," she said, with a frown, as she stared out the window again. "You look back on your teenage years, and it's a blur."

"You know what I think?"

"Please enlighten me," she replied, with mischief in her gaze.

"I think I do remember you," he shared, that smile lighting up his face.

She nodded. "As soon as I mention the eating disorder, everybody knows who I am."

He pondered that, frowning. "Aren't you … weren't you really good at artwork?"

She smiled at him and then nodded. "You do remember me."

"Yeah, I do." He grinned. "I remember thinking that you were damn skinny, and somebody needed to do something about that, but, being a kid, it's not as if any of us knew what to do."

"Right, and being a kid myself, I didn't know what to do either," she added, with a smile. "But you're right. I was very much into my art, and it was a huge plus in my life back then. It was a blessing when it came to recovering, to pull me back out of the eating disorder. My artwork is still my solace, even now."

"Do you still find time?"

"I do, though not as much as I would like to, since I have to work to put food on the table."

"Agreed, but, if you continue to maintain your artwork, maybe something else is out there for you as well."

"There is," she agreed. "I just have to decide how much I'm willing to put into it." At his inquisitive look, she shrugged. "I have a showing coming up in about six months," she whispered, dipping her head, "but, if I think about it, which I do a lot, I get completely queasy and want to call it off."

"Don't do that," he cried out. "If somebody saw enough talent in you for a show, then you need to do the best you can to honor that."

She shook her head. "You're starting to sound like a life coach."

"Maybe that's because I have had a lot of life coaching. You don't come back from war—broken, with a lot of health issues—and snap back, not without talking to people," he shared. "That was how I got back on my feet."

She sipped at her milkshake, as she considered how hard that would have been for Baron. "I think that nobody really sees us as we should see ourselves," she offered.

He nodded. "My brother helped me quite a bit. He just kept living every day, as if it were any other day," he shared, with a smile, "never worrying about whether it would be his last one. Whereas, every time I got out of bed after being injured, it was like this major trauma, and I wasn't sure whether I would ever make it back to the bed or not. Yet he always had a laugh for me, always had a smile, always had encouraging words, basically saying, *Suck it up, buttercup, and get on with it.* Not in those exact words, but that's what he meant."

She burst out laughing. "That doesn't sound terribly encouraging."

"Well, you have to understand our relationship," he added. He went quiet for a moment. "Now I just have my ma."

"Is that good?"

He nodded. "It's good, but it could be better. Like every relationship, I suppose. She's absolutely devastated about losing Brad, which is normal. I don't quite have the same relationship that she had with Brad, so I'm sure a part of her wishes that I had gone instead."

Brittany frowned at him, then leaned forward and grabbed his hand. "I wouldn't even go down that pathway. You can't change the past, but the two of you can now have the relationship that you didn't have before."

He gripped her hand and nodded carefully. "We will, and I hope we will come out of it stronger," he said. "I was gone so much, and they developed a closer relationship. I didn't have that with her, and I certainly didn't have that kind of connection with him, and now he's gone. I didn't get the chance to build that back up again," he shared, "so it's one of those contemplative *life choices* things."

"That's good, and it's also bad," she noted. "Been there, done that, and I can tell you, Baron, it really sucks. When you're on the wrong side of it, it can suck the joy out of everything. But happily you have the time to start anew."

He burst out laughing at the way she had said it, amazed at how easy it was to talk to her. "Won't argue there," he replied. "I mean, definitely some are good times, and some are rougher times, but I'm back in the game, and I'll try to finish what my brother started."

"Well, I hope you find the War Dog."

The waitress interrupted a few minutes later, as she brought over their plates. She looked down at Baron and said, "Enjoy." She then cast a look at Brittany, as if to say, *Ensure you eat,* and it didn't go unnoticed by Baron.

After the waitress left, he raised his eyebrows and whispered to Brittany, "I can see how that would get old very quickly."

"Exactly." She gave a sigh. "On the other hand, I know where she's coming from, and that makes it all good."

"Agreed, but nobody likes to be nagged all the time."

"Nobody likes to be nagged at all," she corrected. "No *all the time* about it. Nobody likes to be nagged, plain and simple."

"Agreed," he admitted. "I'm no different in that respect. An awful lot of things we all try to avoid doing because it causes such a reaction in other people. Yet, in this case, you're doing everything you need to do, and you should be proud of yourself."

She waved her fork at him. "You don't need to build me up like that. I'm fine, you know."

"Good," he replied, as he smiled at her. "Then I don't have to worry about you either because I really don't want to sit here and have to nag you into eating."

She rolled her eyes. "As I told you, that was over years ago."

"I'm really glad to hear that."

"So, nowadays I eat regularly," she stated, "and half the time I'm trying to force my grandma to eat, which is like a role reversal. And let me tell you how it's no fun."

He smiled at that. "Then maybe that's a good thing. It

helps you to understand why you were doing what you were doing, and giving her a better chance of understanding why you were doing what you were doing too."

"I don't think she cares," she declared bluntly. "My grandma is an interesting person, but, at this stage of her life, she is only willing to look at what she wants to look at."

"I think that covers everybody," he noted.

When the bell jingled, indicating somebody else coming through the front door a few minutes later, she didn't bother looking up, until she realized a stillness had come over Baron. She leaned forward. "Okay, so now you need to tell me what is wrong."

He glanced at her and asked discreetly, "Do you know the people who just walked in?"

She looked over at them and shook her head. "No. Should I?"

He shrugged. "They look familiar."

"If you say so," she muttered, "but I don't know them."

"I think they were the men at the Gorman house."

She slowly put down her fork, as she studied the two men. "You mean, the ones who just shot at us?" she asked, her tone turning hard.

He gave her a ghost of a smile and then nodded. "That really upset you, didn't it?"

Her eyebrows shot up, and she nodded fiercely. "Well, yeah. And it should upset you too."

"I'm a little more used to it than you," he pointed out, with an easy laughter in his tone, "but I can understand, if you're not used to being shot at, it's a bit of a shock. You never forget the first time someone takes a potshot at you."

She shook her head. "I certainly hope that is something I never get used to."

"Me too," he agreed, smiling. "So, the answer is still no. You don't know them, right?"

"No, I don't, but you've sure got me thinking about it."

"Don't think too hard, and definitely don't make any sudden movements."

She frowned at him and asked curiously, "You don't think they're dangerous here, do you?"

"I don't know because I don't know what they're up to," he shared, "so take it easy. We're here to eat, so keep at it."

She stared down at the plateful of food she'd been anticipating, but it suddenly looked more like sawdust to her.

He shook his head. "Nope, you need to eat, and that will help keep our cover, assuming they don't know who we are. Just act normal, and all will be well."

"I am so not feeling well right now," she shared, staring at him. "You make it sound as if we're in for a cloak-and-dagger evening."

He nodded. "That we are."

BARON WATCHED THE two men grab a table at the far side of the room, their backs to the wall, and kept watching them as they began to study the other people in the room. He was waiting to gauge the reaction when it was their turn to be scrutinized, and he wasn't disappointed.

As soon as the one man's gaze landed on him, he made brief eye contact and then deliberately let his gaze bounce away, as if he didn't recognize Baron. Yet the other man's response was to lean forward and talk to his partner in a hurried whisper. The two men glanced around, as if they were trying to see if anybody else at the place was concerned.

"Did you do that on purpose?" she asked.

"Yeah," he confirmed. "It's always better to let the enemy know where you are."

"No," she countered in a gasp, "it's definitely better if we *don't* let them know where we are."

He smiled. "But, if I don't tell them where we are, we won't find out where they are, so we can go capture them."

She blinked, as she tried to sort through the meandering path he had just proposed. "Who said we're trying to capture them?" she asked with difficulty. "I would much rather just go home and not get involved in any of this mess."

"You can absolutely do that," he replied. "In fact, I would highly recommend it."

She shook her head, glaring at him. "I'm not leaving you to face them alone."

"Face who?" he asked, giving her a bland smile. "I mean, they don't recognize us, remember?"

"And yet," she began, then fell silent, thinking again how this had become a bad habit for her. The way this evening was going, it was not something she would get rid of soon.

He raised an eyebrow at her. "Were you trying to say something?"

"It doesn't matter whether I was or not," she declared, irritated now, "because you won't listen anyway, will you?"

There was almost a twinkle in her gaze, as if she understood what was going on, yet was hard-pressed to fight it or to even argue it, yet was outraged by it. He chuckled. "You're doing really well, you know."

"I don't feel like I'm doing really well. In fact, I feel like I suck at this."

"There is nothing to suck at," he stated. "This is just us

out for dinner, seeing who and what else is going on around us. Nothing more to do here. We can't be certain that they know who we are."

"Yeah, you say that," she muttered, looking down at her plate, "but it seems to me that you already know the answer to that question."

When his phone buzzed, he pulled it out, looked down, and nodded.

"What's that for?"

"You remember the guy I had you send the license plate to?" He motioned at the food in front of her. "Why aren't you eating? You need to eat."

She glared at him, but he just smiled, picked up his burger, and dove in. It didn't take him very long to polish it off. She had to admit that watching him, calm and cool, was very reassuring on its own. She managed to eat her burger, finishing just a little after him.

He smiled. "You did pretty good justice to that."

"I've always have been able to do that," she said, rolling her eyes. "I would eat, and then I would go exercise, not stopping until I had canceled it out."

He nodded. "That's one way a lot of people control their weight, but taken too far …"

She smiled and nodded. "I was the queen of taking things too far," she admitted, with a groan. "However, I am much better now."

"Good. Let's get the bill, and we'll see what the two guys do."

At that, she winced. "Are we expecting trouble?"

"I'm never expecting trouble, but I'm always prepared for it," he replied, with a bright smile. He caught the attention of the waitress, and she brought the bill for them.

"Are you sure you don't want anything else?"

"No, we're good," he replied, smiling. He paid the bill, making sure he got to it before Brittany could.

She stared at him, giving him a pointed look. "I would have been happy to pay for my meal."

He shrugged. "You can buy next time."

She shook her head. "Cheeky. Very cheeky."

He smiled. "Expedient."

"Right," she said, with an eye roll. "That doesn't make me feel any better."

"It wasn't expected to make you feel anything," he explained, "but I do expect to get you to move."

"Got it," she muttered, "and this is me, moving." As they got outside, she looked back at him. "Are you still worried about them?"

"Not so much worried as interested in them."

"What did that text say? You never did tell me what it was."

"Confirmation on the license plate."

"And?"

He looked at her and shrugged. "The vehicle was stolen."

"Well, good God." She stopped in her tracks.

He nudged her forward. "Get in."

"But it's stolen."

"Yeah, it is, so Badger's contacting the local police."

"And we aren't?"

"Hell no, we aren't," he replied. "We are heading to do something else right now, and that means getting you home, where it's safe and sound." She frowned, and he picked up on that right away. He shook his head at her, "Nope, no frowns."

"Yeah, and what if I like frowning?" she muttered.

He burst out laughing at that. "You do like frowning—and getting in trouble. Yet we have your grandmother and other people here to consider. I don't know what these guys are up to, but there is a limit to how much of this game we can play, without getting the local cops involved."

"I don't want to play *any* games," she grumbled, "and, if they have a stolen vehicle, then they should have been picked up already. Those guys, the cops who were out there, should have snagged them earlier."

"That's a good point, so just think about that for a second and answer me this question. Why didn't they?" He nudged her into his vehicle, slamming the door behind her and making sure that she would buckle up too.

He walked around slowly to his side, glancing into the restaurant to see if the two men were still there. He frowned when he realized they were exiting the café. Hopping into the driver's side, he locked the door and started the engine. She looked at him, picking up his obvious unease.

"You really don't like them, do you?"

"Nope, I sure don't," he stated calmly, "but that doesn't mean I'll run."

"You do know that running isn't a sign of cowardice."

"No, … it sure isn't, but there is a time to run and a time not to run," he said, "and right now is a good time not to run."

"I don't know about that. It seems to be a great time," she muttered. She watched as the men went to their vehicle and hopped in. "Are you expecting them to take off?"

"Yes and no," he replied, looking at the two men discreetly, "I suspect they'll watch us, but I don't want them to follow us to your place."

She froze, gasping as she looked over at him. "Now I didn't need that scenario in my head."

He shrugged. "I didn't think you did, but I'm not one to pussyfoot around if I see a potential problem."

She stared at him, as he slowly pulled out of the parking lot. "Are they behind us?"

"Yeah, they sure are," he said, with another glance into the rearview mirror.

"Do you think I should be texting your friend something?"

"I already did," he shared, with a smile, "but thanks for the offer. Yes, it is definitely something we need to keep an eye on."

"*Great,*" she muttered. They headed back to her place, and she was jittery as hell. "If you're thinking that they'll be a problem, I don't really want you to drop me off."

"That's one of the reasons we're going in this direction," he explained, still keeping an eye behind him. "I want to see if they keep following us. If they take off on their own and don't give a crap, that would be a whole lot better," he added, with a smile in her direction.

"But you're not expecting them to, are you?"

"I am not sure what I'm expecting," he admitted, "but I would also like to know where those two cops are."

She sucked in her breath, as she thought about the implications. "Do you think the gunmen hurt them?"

"It's possible, in which case these two gunmen just escalated whatever they had going on here. They won't get away with attacking two cops, and there will be hell to pay. Plus that attracts a lot of attention."

She sank down a little bit into the seat.

He glanced over at her, chuckling. "Are you trying to

hide from bullets?" he asked.

She winced. "More like I'm trying to hide from the thought of bullets."

"Good idea," he muttered. "I'll do a little bit of roundabout driving here, okay?"

"Oh, please, you do you," she suggested. "I sure don't want two trigger-happy gunmen at my place or to find out where I live."

"Nope, I understand, and, for that consideration alone, I'm hoping it's also possible …"

"What's possible?" she asked, leaning forward to peer into his face. "What is it you're not telling me?"

"I don't want to start something or to even suggest something that could be wrong," he began, "but the other possibility is that they're involved too."

"The cops? No, no, no," she muttered, shaking her head. "We do not want that to be a possibility."

He smiled. "No, we sure don't," he agreed, as he glanced at her, "but that doesn't mean it isn't a possibility."

"They knew Brad though, both of you … right?" she added.

He nodded. "A lot of people around these parts knew him, me less so. Yet that doesn't change anything about who and what these two gunmen are doing up around here. I do feel that I need to go back and ensure the cops are okay."

"Well, in that case," she stated, "you need somebody to go with you."

"Not you," he countered. When she glared at him, he shook his head. "You've had enough of this for the night."

"Maybe," she argued, "but so have you. You've got to be tired, and I know your leg is sore." He looked at her. "You're limping. You're trying not to, but you are."

He shrugged. "Sometimes I have to. The prosthetic can handle things up to a certain point."

"Well, right now is one of the times when it clearly is a bit much." He pulled off to the side of the road.

"Why are you stopping? They'll catch up to us soon. We are sitting ducks here." When he didn't respond, she glared at him. "You are going off to check the Gorman place for those two cops, aren't you? You know you shouldn't go alone."

"I'm fine," he bit off.

She nodded. "Yeah, you're as fine as I am."

He stared at her in astonishment, and then he laughed. "This is the work I do," he told her. "As much as you don't want to hear this, and please don't take it personally, but you'll hold me back."

Her shoulders slumped, as she recognized the truth of his words. "That's not fair," she muttered.

He smiled. "It's nice to know you care, and I appreciate that very much, but—"

"I get it, but you still shouldn't be going out there alone."

"Maybe, but nobody else is trained like I am to do this."

"What is it you're planning on doing?" she asked, looking at him closely.

"First, I'll drop you off, and then I'll head back to ensure there aren't any lost or injured cops down there."

"And yet there shouldn't be any lost cops," she pointed out.

"Right, but I need to confirm that."

She frowned at that. "Do you really think these guys did something to them?"

"I don't know," he admitted, shrugging. He studied the

area around them, waiting in the darkness. He glanced over at her. "Are you okay?"

She nodded. "I am, but I just wish things had turned out differently."

CHAPTER 7

"I CAN WALK back to my place from here, if you want," Brittany offered.

"No," Baron said, "not with these two on our tails and especially not in the dark. I'll ensure that you get home safe," he murmured. He glanced into his rearview mirror, then stiffened ever-so-slightly.

She knew what that meant. "That's them, isn't it?"

"It is. Now let's see what they'll do."

The two guys drove slowly up the road.

She asked, "Do you want me to hide?"

He nodded. "If you don't mind."

She ducked down against the front of the dash, as he slunk down below the windshield, so the gunmen couldn't see him either. "Do you think they saw us?" she asked him.

"No, I don't think so." He glanced around at the neighborhood. "They'll be looking to see if we're here somewhere."

"But it also means that they did come looking for us," she whispered. "Do you think they recognized your truck?"

"A bullet hole is in the side of it, isn't there?"

She gasped. "I never even thought of that."

"Well, it's a good way for them to identify the vehicle, and it's also why I didn't want them to know where you live."

She shook her head, as she watched him from the floor-board. "I can't believe this is what my life has come to."

He shot her a smile. "Hey, it could be worse."

"Yeah, how's that?"

"You could be alone right now."

She winced. "I hadn't even thought of that, but you're right, so thank you." He just waved his hand. "Do you think it's safe to pop up yet?"

"Not yet. I'm waiting to see if they'll get out and walk the area."

"Oh no, that wouldn't be good," she muttered. "I don't like the idea of that at all."

"Which is why we'll stay right where we are and see what they do. They've pulled over to the shoulder and are parked ahead of us."

"Shit," she muttered. She couldn't see anything, hidden as she was. To top it off, it was very sense depriving. The truck was old and smelly. "Is this Brad's truck?"

He looked at her and smiled. "It is."

"You took your brother's truck?"

"I didn't think he would need it anymore," he pointed out mildly, "and it's the perfect vehicle for the work I'm doing."

"I'm sorry. I didn't mean it that way."

"It's fine," he replied. "People say all sorts of things when they're in these situations."

"How often have you been in these situations?" she asked, looking over at him. "So often that you can under-stand people's reactions?"

"Yep. I've seen a lot," he stated.

She stared at him. "I think there are a lot of ghosts in your history."

He glanced at her and then nodded. "Yeah, I suppose there are, but part of rebuilding my life was making sure I didn't bring the ghosts with me."

"Is that possible?"

"I hope so," he declared. Then he whispered, "Hold on. They're getting out."

"Crap," she muttered. "I feel the need to run, but I've got no place to go."

"No, we won't run," he murmured. "Worst case, I'll drive away and leave them staring after us."

"But that will let them know that we're aware of what they're doing."

"Yep," he replied shrewdly, "and that's the nature of this cat-and-mouse game. I would just as soon have the upper hand and not let them know it just yet, if we don't have to."

She nodded and then buried her face in her hands.

He gripped her shoulder. "It'll be okay."

She nodded, turning slightly to look at him. "Says you." But she noticed that his gaze was centered outside, and she had to wonder how much he could see. "What are they doing now?"

"They're walking the block," he shared, "but they're going away from us. I suspect they'll come around on the far side, so they can keep an eye on where we are, without looking like they're searching for us."

"Crap," she muttered.

Just then his phone rang, and he quickly answered it. She listened in, as he talked to Badger.

"Yes," he murmured, "it's the same vehicle. Two cops apparently went to the site where we were earlier and talked with Brittany. They supposedly went looking for me, but I've seen no sign of them. That's why I want to make a trip back to the Gorman place to ensure those cops are okay. I'm not sure what these two armed clowns are up to, but I doubt that simple looting is at the heart of it, although it could be."

"It depends whose properties may be available to be looted," Badger noted.

Hearing that, Brittany poked her head up and stared at him in shock.

"Hang on a minute, Badger. Brittany, that means something to you. What is it? Why did you react like that?"

"Well, I …"

"Nope, not a good time to stop the conversation."

She groaned. "It's just that one of the houses down there, the owner was a suspected murderer from years and years ago. He was also involved in gang-related things, stealing high-end stuff. Maybe he killed somebody during a robbery. Several in the gang got caught for some heists, but this one owner didn't."

Baron stared at her for a long moment. "Are you talking about the Galloway gang?"

She nodded. "One of the gang owned a home right next to the spooky Gorman house. You did hear how Gorman spent time in jail too, right? What if Gorman was working with the Galloway gang? I have nothing to support that obviously, but with two criminals living next door, that seems to be an easy leap."

"Right. The gunmen were near both houses. But, as you said, we don't know which house they were possibly searching. Could be both, for all we know. That changes everything. Badger, did you hear that?" Baron asked. Hearing whatever Badger said on the other end, Baron put his cell on Speaker. "Repeat what you just told me to Badger, will you?"

Brittany quickly repeated what she had told Baron, with Badger firing questions at her.

"Did you ever see anybody there at the Galloway gang's home?"

"I haven't myself, but my grandmother has. I wouldn't know because the place is a bit farther down that road from me and out of the way. However, people have been living there for years. I just never really knew who they were, whether they had people moving on, others moving in, or it's just an empty place now," she muttered.

"Any idea what the address is?" Badger asked.

"No, I don't, … but it's maybe six or seven houses past my grandma's, just around the corner of the block there. You have to turn the corner, and then it was one of those big houses right along there," she said. "I don't know which one exactly from here. I could figure it out if I was there, but I don't know it from memory."

"But you could pick it out on a satellite map?" Baron asked.

"Oh, yeah, that I can do."

"Okay, we'll do that, and I'll get back to you," Baron told Badger. "Seems some continued gang activity could be going on here."

Badger added, "Definitely could be."

As soon as Badger ended the call, Brittany frowned at Baron, confused as hell. "Why now? The murder was at least a decade ago. If the original Galloway gang was involved in somebody's death but were otherwise a bunch of thieves, why would they resurface now? What difference would any of it make now?"

"Maybe they were in jail for a time. Maybe the hurricane made a difference if they were afraid something would be revealed with all the destruction."

She stared at him. "That makes a sick sense, and I really don't want to think about it."

"Then don't," he invited. "Come on. Let's go."

"Where are we going now?" she asked. "What about our gunmen?"

"I don't care about those guys," he stated. "We're leaving." He started up the engine, pulled out into the street, and, making a U-turn, disappeared down the block.

"What are they doing?" she asked.

"Running to their vehicle," he replied calmly.

"Well, … crap," she muttered. "Are you sure you want to do this?"

"I am because Badger knows where we are, where we are going, and he's sending in some backup for us," he muttered. "I'm just not sure what we're dealing with here, but we need to sort it out fast. Now I'm really worried about the local cops who were down there searching for me."

"They were both young, very young. I knew the one, but I can't remember what his name was."

He looked over at her. "Maybe your grandmother would know?"

"Maybe, but it's too late now. And even if she were awake I don't really want to call her because I don't want to answer her million questions."

He laughed. "Just something about grandmothers, isn't there? It's really hard to fob them off when they want to know something."

"Absolutely, and explain to me why you can't just lie to them and get away with it? I don't understand what magic that is."

Still grinning, he nodded. "Maybe it's something that

you could ask her though and see if she knows anything about them. Or is there anybody else who would help you recognize them?"

"Your brother would have been the go-to guy. He was helpful in all kinds of ways."

Baron smiled. "That would be Brad, the hometown hero."

She chuckled. "I'm pretty sure you don't get a pass on that one either. Why is it nobody ever likes to be called a hero?"

"I don't think anybody particularly objects to it," he explained, with a mocking look in her direction. "It's all about how it's intended. Heroes are around us every day, but they are common everyday heroes, and that was my brother. He would go mow the neighbor's yard or go grocery shopping for someone's grandma."

"That's right. He did. I forgot that part."

"He used to take our mother out and get her hair done every once in a while, just so she would have a better day," Baron shared. "Brad was just one of those guys who was inherently kind, and he didn't think about himself as much as he thought about others."

"Which is also why he's dead," she pointed out.

He nodded. "Maybe."

"Maybe?" she repeated, turning to look at him.

He shrugged. "He was out trying to rescue dogs scattered by the storm, so, yes, that was one of the things that put him into the grave."

"Why do I sense more behind that than you're letting on?"

He shook his head. "Nope, I'm not looking for conspiracy theories where there aren't any," he replied. "But I am looking to confirm those young policemen are okay."

"Well, you're not leaving me behind, not after we know that the two gunmen are still chasing us down," she declared.

"I know." He nodded. "I changed my mind when I realized they were following us."

"Good." Then she groaned. "Shit. That means I'm heading back in there with you."

He laughed. "Either that or you'll go to Camille's place, where your grandmother is."

"No, I don't want to bring trouble to them either. Those two ladies are definitely characters, and most likely they would be up for the thrill, but they don't need this kind of trouble."

"I understand, and I wouldn't want to bring this to my mother's place either. Still, I'm not happy to get you involved."

"I've already been involved," she muttered, "so how about you find a way to get me uninvolved?"

"Well, I would love to, but that would mean solving the whole thing."

"Done," she declared. "That's the best answer. I don't want to come back down here and start searching through my grandma's stuff if we've got some wild cards like these armed men, running around, raising hell all over the place."

"Agreed." He looked over at her and smiled. "See? That was pretty easy."

"Yeah, but … you're leading me in directions that I'm really not prepared to go."

"I'm not leading you anywhere," he clarified. "I just want to ensure that you're safe."

"I want that too, but, if this will continuously hound me, then let's solve it, once and for all. That way I'll know that my grandma and Camille are safe too, not to mention everybody else who will already have their hands full trying to rebuild their lives. It's just complete shit that something like this has to happen right now, especially when we're already dealing with so much pain and loss."

"I agree," he murmured, "but it doesn't change the fact that people will take advantage of the situation. We have seen this time and time again, and the minute there's an opening, the bad guys are right there."

"That just means they're assholes," she stated bluntly.

"I won't argue that one," he murmured, "but it doesn't change the facts, though."

"No, maybe not, but I wish it did." They drove in silence for a few minutes, and she looked over at him. "Are you sure there's no conspiracy theory going on in your head?"

"I'm sure," he replied, then studied his rearview mirror.

"They're after us again, aren't they?" she asked, with a groan.

"Well, let's just say that somebody is behind us."

"Damn it," she muttered. "Is it even safe to go back there? It seems to me that we are heading right into their turf."

"No, it sure isn't safe," he conceded. "That's why I want police backup, particularly if nobody has seen the first two cops."

"Wouldn't it make sense to check and see if they made it home already, safe and sound?"

"Badger already did, and nobody's seen them for some time."

"But apparently nobody is exactly worried either, and that's a little concerning," she pointed out. "Why wouldn't the other cops all be out looking for them?"

"Because, at the moment, we know nothing. The police don't know that they have two cops in trouble. As a matter of fact, they don't know shit."

"Except you do," she said, eyeing him carefully.

He hesitated, then nodded. "Yes, I do."

"And you think nobody'll believe you?"

"I don't know whether they will or not," he stated calmly, "but, without proof, it'll be a little hard to sort out, won't it?"

"Maybe," she muttered, "but if it's the wrong men …"

He smiled. "The police have to know for sure that their men are in trouble before they go call out others on a wild goose chase, especially when they are already spread thin just trying to keep all these places secure from looters."

"And yet … you don't think this is about looting, do you?"

He glanced at her and replied, "No, I don't."

BARON DIDN'T KNOW what to do with Brittany.

He didn't want her with him because it was too dangerous, and she was already fighting that. However, he also knew that he couldn't just drop her off back home again, not with these gunmen following them, at least for the moment. He wondered whether his brother had run into any of this or it was completely unrelated. "You never saw the War Dog anywhere, did you?" He kept his eyes on the road ahead, periodically checking behind him.

"Not enough to know that it was there." He just stayed quiet. "Yet we heard that bark earlier."

He nodded. "I went looking for it, but I couldn't find the source."

"Do you think the gunmen had something to do with the War Dog?"

"If they did, he's probably just been locked up in order to give them access, if he was getting in their way."

"They wouldn't hurt him, would they?"

"I hope not," he stated bluntly, "but, if any dog gives them trouble, no doubt they'll just shoot him. If they can shoot a person, shooting a dog is no big deal to them. I'm really hoping they won't and that they don't see the dog as being in their way."

"That's the first thing I want to check," she muttered, as they drove along to where they'd been shot at the last time. "And second, are the police still there?"

"We will definitely do that, but, if injured cops are up here, we have to find them and get them out."

Brittany sighed. "I just came down to find a few family heirlooms for my grandma—and to find Pocket of course."

"Well, you found Pocket," he said, shooting her a big grin, "and the rest just fell into place."

"If that's what you call falling into place." She fell silent, as Baron navigated past the tree that he had dropped to slow the gunmen's progress. "Do you think it slowed them down at all?"

"Depends on if they took another way around it," he replied. "I was wondering that myself."

"It's a little freaky to think they got out of here so easily the last time. There had to be another outlet."

"It's quite possible that's exactly what they did," he murmured, as he looked over at her. "Remember that, so far, these guys aren't acting normal."

"No, they aren't, and I can't stand that because I'm always second-guessing what's going on here."

"Well, maybe somebody up here was involved in hiding something. Maybe the hurricane started something or maybe interrupted it or uncovered it. The gunmen may be checking on the Gorman house or the Galloway gang house, checking on their stash, deciding if it's a good time to divvy up the assets," he suggested.

"Right," she muttered. "Greed always kicks in, doesn't it?"

"Greed always kicks in," he confirmed, with a nod. "It's pretty hard to get away from it. If these guys are criminals, you can bet they'll be looking for an opportunity to make something happen in their world, and this hurricane may have given them that opening."

Brittany snorted. "It would sure be nice to not deal with this crap right now."

"That would be a dream," he muttered, with a smile in her direction. "So dream on as much as you want to, just don't let it color your logical thinking." He slowed down, as they pulled up to the front of one of the houses. "I had made it this far when I heard the dog." He shut off the engine, and they sat in the silence.

"What about the people behind us?"

"We lost them back there," he said, "but I suspect they won't be too far behind."

"Great," she muttered. Just then he perked up, and, at the same time, she straightened. "Was that a dog? I heard something, but I'm not sure."

"I swear to God it's the same dog," he muttered but hesitated to leave her.

She shooed him away. "Go."

He frowned at her and shook his head. "I can't leave you here alone."

"Damn it, I guess we're both going then." With half a laugh, she hopped out on her side. "Let's just keep the boogeymen away, please."

"As far as I know, they didn't follow us down this far," he shared. "We also don't know for sure it was them."

"That's a damn lie," she declared. "You have a very good idea who it is. You just don't want me to make the same connection." Even in the darkness, she could see the whites of his eyes as he smiled. "See? I'm not a dumb bunny," she muttered.

"I would never insult you by suggesting such a thing." He laughed softly. Then they heard the bark again. "Let's move."

Using a flashlight to guide their way, he headed down to where the barking came from. As they got closer, the dog fell silent.

"Why do they do that?" she asked, irritated, "I mean, it got us here, and now it's as if …" Then she whispered, "It's almost as if it's a trap."

He glanced over at her. "Not exactly what we want to think about right now."

"Maybe not, but that's what I feel screaming at me."

He brushed her behind him and whispered, "Stay back."

She nodded. "I'm not planning on being a hero."

"Good," he muttered. As they headed down the debris-filled street, everything was in darkness.

"How can we even tell how much of the house is still standing?"

"Not much is left of this one. One of the side walls has come down, and part of the building itself has collapsed."

"Do you think the dog is trapped?"

"It's a possibility," he murmured. "I'll see if I can get close enough to tell."

As he walked a little farther, keeping her right behind him, she whispered, "You don't want to call out to him?"

He glanced back and smiled. "I'm thinking about it potentially being a trap." He squeezed her hand and added, "I'll call out to him when I get a little closer, but I don't want to alert anybody else."

"Right," she muttered, "that *everybody else* thing again." She glanced behind them but saw no sign of anyone. Yet why would there be? They were the ones with a flashlight. They were the ones lighting the way, but Baron was all focused on the dog again. So was she to a certain extent, but she also wanted to know where Anthony, she finally remembered the name of the one cop, and his buddy were.

As they came around the side of the house, part of the roof was on the ground.

"I tell you these hurricanes are tough on the roofs," she muttered.

"They are," he agreed. He circled the area with his flashlight, then he froze.

She gasped because right there in front of them was one of the young cops, tied up and seemingly unconscious. "It's Anthony."

She raced forward, but he grabbed her and held back. "Just a minute. … He's unconscious. We'll have to be careful with this. The thing is, I doubt he was left without a guard."

She froze in place and turned to look at him, her heart in her chest. "Well then, we need to get him out of here fast. This poor guy's been here for hours."

He nodded. "And, with any luck, he's just fine."

"We don't know that."

"I need to ensure that we're safe, so we can get the word out. You stay here, and let me do a quick search around. We also have to find that dog." He did a quick circle around and then nodded as he came toward the young cop. He bent down and pulled the gag off his mouth and checked him over. "He appears unhurt."

With a jerk, the cop opened his eyes and tried to speak, finally opening his mouth and whispering, "What happened?"

"You were attacked." Brittany squatted beside him. "Give us a chance to untie you, and then you'll have to move slowly because you'll be incredibly stiff and sore."

Baron freed him and gently moved the cop's arms. Anthony groaned. At that, Baron slowly lifted him to his feet. "This may seem out of context, but I'm looking for a dog, a dog we're trying to help. We've heard a dog around here somewhere. Have you seen him? Every time I get close enough, he bolts."

"Yeah, we saw a dog, but we couldn't get near it. It does seem terrified," Anthony replied.

"Was it a shepherd?" Baron asked.

"Maybe. The dog I saw was black, big, mean-looking as if he'd had some rough years."

"The dog I'm looking for is a War Dog that had more than a few rough years in the military and was now looking for an easier time of it."

"I don't know about an easier time of it. This dog appeared to have had a rough few years, or maybe just the last few weeks anyway," he muttered. "That could be. I don't know." He massaged his wrists and then rubbed his temples. "My head is killing me right now."

"What happened to your partner?" Baron asked him.

"I don't know," he said, as he looked around. "I don't know what happened." He reached up, then groaned as he touched his head. "Shit, I tell you my head, … it's on fire or something."

Baron took a quick look and announced, "Yeah, we'll have to get you into the hospital and get that stitched up."

"Stitched up?" he asked, staring at Baron.

"Yeah, you've taken a serious blow to your head." He pulled out his phone and quickly phoned Badger.

"Who is Badger, and why are you calling him?" Anthony asked in confusion.

"Because I know that he'll contact your outfit," Baron explained, "and that's about the fastest way we can pull this together and get you out of here." He didn't worry about any other explanations.

In the distance, they heard the dog bark again, and Anthony perked up. "That's him."

"Was he hurt?" Baron asked.

He nodded. "He was hurt, and he had something around his neck that was hurting him more."

A shadow passed over Baron's face as he turned to Brittany. "I need the two of you to stay here. I'll keep looking around."

"Wait," she cried out. He turned, and she spoke fast, too fast, as if she wouldn't get another chance. "Please wait until the cops get here. Then you can go look for the dog. Besides, we're already missing one cop here. Don't go."

"I understand, and I'll be looking for him as well as the dog," he explained. "Both are important, and I'm not sure that we'll get another chance to do this. And, if his partner is hurt too, we need to get him out of here." Baron turned to

Anthony and asked, "What is his name?"

"Josh. I don't know what happened to him. Hell, I don't know what happened to me."

Baron looked from Anthony back to her. "Stay here." With that, he disappeared into the darkness.

He moved through the shadows silently, not sure who the enemy was at this point. Unsure whether it was the gunmen on his tail or somebody else altogether.

Hearing the dog bark one more time, Baron completely shifted his orientation and then moved quickly through the darkness, until he came upon the dog, sitting, partially trapped by debris, yet looking like he may free himself. Baron called out softly, "Kingston, is that you?"

The War Dog started to whine and howl, hearing his name.

Baron walked closer and bent down to get a huge greeting. Using his flashlight, he checked to see how badly the dog was hurt. Definitely some blood was on his shoulder and some on his back, but neither injury appeared to be impeding him. However, the rope that seemed to be both a collar and a lead on his neck was definitely restricting him. The rope appeared to be snagged by the debris. Baron moved around some of the wood and limbs and shingles off the dog's back legs, then quickly cut the rope, and Kingston danced free.

With the War Dog free and clear, Baron surveyed his surroundings and muttered, "Now where is the other cop?"

At that, Kingston barked once and took off running. With the uneven ground, the stacks of debris left by the hurricane, and the challenges caused by Baron's leg, it was difficult to keep up with the dog. By the time he reached the dog's side again, Kingston was barking at another stack of various materials in front of him.

"Is he in here, boy?" Bending down, he took a closer look and, sure enough, found a cop, once again tied up and stuck under some debris to hide him. "Well, crap."

The dog started sniffing around, licking the cop's face.

Baron asked, "Do you know this one?"

Kingston barked.

The cop groaned, opened his eyes, and started to panic.

This must be Josh. Baron bent down and calmed him. "Hey, hold still. I'm here for the rescue," he explained. "Let's not bring all this down on top of us, okay? I'm not the bad guy."

"Who are you?"

"Baron. I've got your partner a couple houses away," he shared. "No need to worry. Anthony is okay but for a hard knock on the head. Let's get you untied so I can get you onto your feet and get some circulation moving."

Realizing that he wasn't the enemy, the cop whispered, "My name's Josh." His voice was cracked and hoarse. "I don't suppose you have any water."

"Not on me," Baron noted, "but we'll get you some soon. Let's get going, and we'll head back to Anthony." When he got the cop up, Baron realized that Josh had a leg injury and wouldn't be walking anywhere. "Did they do this to you?"

"Yeah, but I don't know who it was," he muttered. "They came out of nowhere. We were searching the area because of the looters. We'd been talking to a woman who told us that somebody was out here, trying to stop looters."

"Well, that was me, and I wasn't trying to stop looters, but I was trying to see what those guys were up to. Plus I was looking for this War Dog."

"I was hit from behind and didn't get a chance to defend myself," he muttered. "It's as if they were expecting us."

"And that could be true. You can't walk out of here on that leg."

Josh was limping badly and clearly dehydrated. No point denying that when they were all in trouble.

"Sorry, man. I'll just wait here until you can get somebody to wheel me out."

Baron smiled. "Well, that'll take a bit, and, if you haven't noticed, the roads are quite a mess."

"What will you do then?"

"I'll get you down there with the others. I want you all in one place, so I don't have to keep splitting my energy off, finding everybody," he shared, with a half laugh.

"Agreed, but I don't think I can walk much farther."

"No, so we'll have to do it the hard way." With that, he bent down and picked him up in a fireman's carry. "Let me know if it gets to be too much."

They were well underway when his phone buzzed with a text from Badger. He quickly set Josh against a tree, dug out his Bluetooth earpiece, and placed a quick call to Badger.

"Have you got an update for me?"

"Yeah, I've got the other cop, but he's hurt, so I'm having to pack him. With all the rubble, it's pretty slow going, but I've got to get back to the others." With that, he pocketed his phone, the call still live, and picked Josh back up again, with an audible grunt.

"Sounds like Kat needs to do a revamp on that leg joint," Badger noted, with his customary amusement in his tone. "I'm pretty sure she has a load restriction on it."

"Then she needs to raise it," he muttered, as he picked his way slowly back. He whistled once, and Kingston came to his side. "Oh, and I found the dog."

"You did?" Badger perked up. "Really?"

"Yeah, he's right here beside me. I still have to check the chip, but he's responding to his name when I call him *Kingston*."

"We have to be sure," Badger said.

"If my arms weren't full, and it wasn't so dark out here, I would send you a photo," he replied, trying his best to steady his breathing, "but it looks to be him."

"Now that is good news," Badger said warmly. "Much better than the rest of your situation."

CHAPTER 8

B RITTANY STARED RESENTFULLY at the gunman who had come up on her and Anthony, leaving her no time to even scream or to react in any way.

"Wow, wow, wow, look at that. Anthony got free."

Anthony just stared at him, angry, and she realized that this must be one of the gunmen who had tied him up in the first place.

Damn it all, they were back to square one. "What are you doing?" she asked, blustering. "We need help getting him to a hospital. He's injured."

"Yeah, he probably is," the stranger replied, taunting her. He wore a dark sweatshirt with the hood pulled up over his head, so it was almost impossible to see his face. "But since I had the pleasure of inflicting those injuries, it's not likely I'll be helping him."

She gasped in horror, hoping he would believe her act. "Why would you do that? He's never done anything to you. Why would you hurt him?"

"How do you know he's never done anything to me?" he asked, looking at her. "That's a hell of an assumption to make."

She stared at him. "You're right," she muttered, "I don't know why I thought that. I just assumed you were out here being mean."

He laughed. "Well, yes, I am. It's part of my charm," he said, with a snarl in her direction. "But that's okay. I'm just waiting for the rest of your party. Until we have everybody all in one place, I guess you're safe, at least for a few minutes. After that? … No promises."

Her heart sank. No way to hide the fear that suddenly swept over her, and the gunman would know it too, as it would definitely show up on her face.

He laughed. "That's right." He gave her a smile. "Anthony here got it once already, and his buddy is around here somewhere. So, if you think you'll try anything, you have another think coming. You better be careful from here on out. Every move you make, you think about the consequences," he threatened, his tone turning low and deadly, "because I'll shoot you, just as easily as I'll shoot them."

"Them?" she repeated. "Did you hurt his partner?"

"Yes, I hurt his partner," he confirmed in that same deadly tone, "and you don't see anybody out here rushing to their rescue, do you?"

She froze at that but still asked, "Why not?"

"Shit, is that all you do, ask questions?"

"You have to admit you started with a pretty strong opening," she muttered. "So why wouldn't I be asking questions? Why aren't the police down here helping them?"

"Because they don't know he's missing, for one thing."

Anthony at her side muttered, "Because his brother used to be a cop." He spat on the ground.

"So, is your brother a part of this too?" she asked the gunman.

"*Nah*, he's not part of anything. Besides, he's far too uptight to be a part of this. He hates the shit Anthony gets into. They barely talk anymore. Anthony, you should know that by now. No wonder you're still just on foot patrol, even after all this time."

"Doesn't matter whether I know it or not," Anthony argued. "When you get attacked by people you know, it makes you second-guess everything."

"Not a bad thing to second-guess the shit you're doing in your life, Anthony. I mean, did you really think you would just blast through life and not have to pay for your father's sins?"

"My father's sins, not mine," Anthony snapped. "I didn't have anything to do with the shit he did."

It was hard to see the age of the man in front of them, but he had a seedier tone to his voice, as if he'd been through more in life than she had. She looked from one man to the other. "I'm a little confused," she admitted, "and considering that I'm in trouble here because of trying to help Anthony, I would like to know what's going on." She kept her tone as stiff as she could, as if she were more interested in what was going on, than the actual thought of being in trouble here, all the while hoping Baron could find them in time.

The hooded man just laughed. "I don't give a shit if you're curious," he snarled, "and Anthony may be prepared to tell you about his father and his history, but I'm not," he muttered. "And why should I anyway? I've got better things to do than answer your shitty little questions."

She turned to look at Anthony, the young cop beside her, and he shrugged. "My dad's a piece of shit," he muttered, "and it doesn't seem to matter how much we try to get rid of his influence because it keeps coming back on us."

"But it's what your father did, not you." She frowned at Anthony and asked curiously, "What's your last name?"

"It doesn't matter," he muttered.

She thought about it and then added, "I don't suppose your dad is connected to that Galloway gang case that was never solved a while back, was he? The one where he was allegedly part of that treasure hunt?"

Anthony stared at her, as the gunman laughed. "See? Look at the notoriety in your world," the gunman said. "Even some dumb chick from town knows about it."

"It doesn't matter whether I heard about it or not," she replied. "You know how it is with rumors that have been around forever."

"Yeah, well some rumors have a basis of truth," the gunman muttered, "and this guy had better be willing to cough up the truth. Otherwise there will be hell to pay. Understand, Anthony?"

"Why don't you go ask his father?" she suggested.

"I would love to have a chat with Daddy dearest, but here's the snag. ... I can't. Daddy dearest is gone, poof, dusted."

"Okay, and what about the rest of his partners in crime?"

The gunman barked at her, "Some things we just can't get answers for."

Staring at him, she had barely opened her mouth when he snapped at her again.

"No more. Just stop with the fifty questions. How about you just shut the fuck up and sit there. I've heard enough of your prattling. You don't know what you're talking about, and nobody here will explain it to you, so just shut up."

"Or what?"

And, with that, he turned and pivoted back, pointing the gun directly at her. "Or else."

BARON CAREFULLY NAVIGATED his way back, one house at a time, still on the call with Badger. "Ah, shit."

"What?" Badger asked, refocusing on the issue at hand.

"I hear voices, and I don't like the sound of what's being said."

"Of course not. Stash the cop and go in carefully. You know the drill," Badger muttered, then disconnected.

Baron did know the drill, and, looking around, he found what appeared to be an old cot sitting off to the side, tossed away by the hurricane. He laid Josh on it, trying not to cause any more damage than what had already been done to the young man. Not even a moan came out of him, despite the pain it must have caused. "Damn, I'm sorry," Baron muttered, as he straightened up.

The other man didn't make a sound.

Whispering a command to Kingston, Baron turned in the direction the voices were coming from and carefully crept forward, trying to avoid stumbling through the debris. Staying out of sight, he got close enough to hear. Then, peeking around the corner from his new position, he saw a single gunman standing over Brittany.

"Or else I will pop you one. I told you to shut the fuck up, and I won't tell you again."

Baron winced as the gun was raised and pointed straight at her, while Brittany stood there, still glaring at the man.

Anthony, the young cop with the head injury, called out from his position on the ground, "You don't need to shoot her, for God's sake. It's not as if we can fight."

"No, but she won't shut up."

"Well, she probably will now," Anthony replied.

The gunman stared at the two of them and then made an angry noise.

"You can get the hell out of here as soon as you tell me where my partner is," Anthony declared, without missing a beat.

Silence came from all around them. Baron hadn't seen any sign of another man out here but knew there had been two of them earlier. So, where the hell was that partner?

"I didn't even know you had a partner out here," Brittany exclaimed, her tone loud and strong.

Baron smiled. First, it meant she wasn't injured, and, second, she had just enough of that pissed-off attitude in her tone that he was even happier to hear it. She wouldn't go down and stay down. She wouldn't go down without a fight. She just had to ensure she picked her fights in a way that didn't get her killed in the process. Of course that went for everybody, and, right now, this was a bad deal for anyone.

"Yeah," the gunman grumbled, "I'm looking for my partner, and I don't like the fact that you're out here, nosing around, when no one is supposed to be around this place to begin with."

"Well, if we'd known you were here," she stated in exasperation, "and you'd put up a sign to stay away or something, we might have."

"No, you wouldn't," he argued, giving her an angry look. "You're one of those lousy do-gooders out here, pissing everybody off all the time."

She fell silent at that, and, for Baron, it was just another insight into her character. Maybe she did know when to stand and when to fall because, right now, she appeared to be considering her options.

"Well, at least you've shut up now," he muttered.

She didn't say anything, but it was obvious that something had started to build.

Baron slipped around, checking out the location, wondering where the hell the other gunman was. The last thing Baron needed was to be caught with yet another person out here and not know who and what was going on.

"I don't know where your partner is," she finally said, "but I sure hope he's not hurting out here. It's pretty empty, and it's dark, and a hell of a lot of debris is everywhere."

"I know that," the gunman snapped. "Tell me something I don't know."

She shrugged. "Well, the cops will probably be here any minute."

"Why?"

Baron just caught a corner of the movement, as the gunman turned, apparently unaware they had gotten calls out.

"Because I called them," she stated in exasperation. "I mean, I found an injured cop, after all. Anthony was so out of it, injured and tied up, plus the other cop is missing. What else could I do?"

The gunman swore, loudly and profusely. "You're just nothing but trouble," he snapped, his gaze searching, trying to figure out something. As if he was on the verge of a panic, he raised his gun and fired in the air, and then he fired aimlessly. Brittany ducked, whereas Anthony had no chance to move, but the bullets flew in a circle around him.

Baron ducked but kept an eye on the scene. When silence fell, he straightened up to see that the gunman had disappeared. As a way to gain cover, it wasn't bad. Yet, when he heard a motor starting up off to the side, Baron swore and ran in that direction, but it was too dark. And, with no lights on, the vehicle took off harmlessly, just to the side of him. Swearing, he raced back to where Brittany was crouched beside Anthony. "Hey," Baron murmured. "Are you guys okay?"

"We're okay," she muttered, looking up at him, "but if you'd been here just a minute earlier …"

He nodded. "I was just coming in, and I heard part of the conversation, but I couldn't get into position to do anything about it." Baron glared down the road. "Badger is on the hunt too."

"Well, that won't do us any good though. Isn't he in New Mexico?" she asked, glaring at him.

"Never underestimate the guy. He is a wizard when it comes to support. Plus the other cops are on the way too," he added, "but I don't know if we'll stop this guy."

"Not likely," Anthony muttered, hanging his head.

"Why is that?"

He shrugged. "None of our cops are great at rescue. Nobody's got any training really. No budget money. While everybody wants everything, they don't want to pay for it," he muttered. "At the last council meeting, it was brought up that there had been very little search and rescue training and that the police officers needed more, but the council denied the request, saying we had no need for that because nobody here ever got injured."

When she snorted at that, he nodded. "Wish they lived out here near my grandma's place."

"I get it. You have no idea what it's like when you're up against people and budgets," Anthony muttered. "All they want to do is spend money on their pet projects, but nobody wants to spend money on health and safety." He turned and looked back at Baron. "We still don't know what happened to my partner, Josh."

"I've got him nearby. He's alive, but I don't want to

move him too much, not until we see what his injuries are. I already carried him a house or so over from here."

At that, Anthony got up and slowly walked toward him. "Show me."

He led them to where the other cop was unconscious.

"Damn." Anthony approached Josh. "He really is out, isn't he?"

"He sure is," Baron confirmed. "You both took blows to the head, and Josh has a bum leg."

"Caught us by surprise," Anthony admitted, "I didn't see anything. One second I am walking, and, the next thing I know, I'm seeing stars. It was so dark out too. They must have had night vision goggles because he didn't seem to be hampered the same way we were."

"Night vision goggles sounds about right," Baron replied. "Military issue is pretty easy to get online, anytime you want nowadays." He bent over, double-checking the officer on the makeshift bed, before turning to look at Brittany. "Are you okay?"

"I am," she replied, with a smile in his direction, "I'm glad you found Josh." Just then, Kingston walked over stiffly and put his nuzzle into her hand. "Oh my gosh," she cried out, as she crouched to say hello. Kingston got a happy greeting. She looked over at Baron. "You didn't send him after the gunman?"

He shook his head. "No, I didn't know where the gunman's partner was, and we didn't know for sure how many bad guys we were even dealing with, until he mentioned his missing partner," Baron explained. "So I didn't want the dog to get shot, considering how trigger-happy our gunman got earlier."

"He was, and that was crazy," she noted, "and not a

whole lot you could have done without a weapon yourself."

She kept harping on that, and it was pissing off Baron, but, from her point of view, he could also understand the sentiment. Honest to God, he felt that way himself to a certain extent. His priority had to be keeping them safe, so going after the armed bad guy in the dark wasn't the right move. He looked back over at Anthony. "How are you feeling?"

"Like crap, and even more so after seeing Josh." Anthony motioned at his partner. "He told me to stay put, but I was bound and determined that we could do a quick search and go home. I didn't listen, and now he's hurt too."

"Hopefully it's not as bad as it could be," Baron replied. "However, if the backup doesn't show up soon, I think I should just pick him up and take him down to the hospital."

"I thought you didn't want to move him."

"I don't, but it's not doing him any good to just lay out here. Plus he's already been moved. I'm not sure what is the lesser of the evils at this point," he muttered, "but I saw no broken bones. It'll take a CT scan to sort it out."

"We don't have anything like that here," Anthony pointed out, "so you'll have to go to a bigger hospital."

"And that's why we have ambulances."

"Except that no ambulance will come down here," Anthony pointed out, and it stung. "This is no-man's land right now, and nobody is supposed to even be here," he stated, shooting them a glance.

"Ah, well, if that dirty look was for my benefit," Brittany replied, rolling her eyes, "I've just been here trying to find some of my grandma's things."

"And yet," the cop added, his tone turning harsh, "it's not just you here, is it? It brought us down here too."

"No," she snapped, glaring at him. "It's these assholes who were obviously up to no good who got you called out here, not us."

He shrugged. "Well, if everybody would stay out of these zones when they're supposed to," he explained, chewing on his words, "we wouldn't have gotten hurt either."

"Maybe, but saying nobody's allowed to be here didn't make a damn bit of difference to that son of a bitch."

Anthony nodded. "That's very true. I'm just pissed off and fed up, and I've got one hellacious headache."

Just enough petulance filled his tone for her to smile and look over at Baron.

Baron nodded. "Considering we won't get the help that I was hoping for, I think we need to take Josh to the hospital and get both of you checked over. I would feel better if he would wake up."

Almost as if understanding what the difficulty was, a groan came from Josh.

Anthony perked up. "Thank God." With a bright smile, he bent over his buddy. "Wake up. Come on. Wake up, buddy."

It took a few minutes before Josh opened his eyes, and he stared around at them. "What happened?"

"Lots, none of it good," his partner replied. "I'm sorry. It's my fault."

Josh looked at him for a long moment and frowned. "Did we get sucker punched or something?"

"Pretty much," he admitted, "and they're gone, but we survived."

"Are you hurt too?"

"I got taken out," he admitted, "something I'm not terribly proud of."

"I don't give a shit about feeling proud about it," Josh replied, barely coherent. "We're alive, right?" He slowly sat up and swore. "Damn, my head."

"Yeah, they apparently clobbered both of us over the head. Plus you've got a bum wheel too, according to this guy." Then he provided a shortened version of events to bring him up to speed with what was going on.

By the time Josh understood the situation as well, he turned to look at them. "Let's get out of here. I don't feel like anything's broken, but I do need to get my head checked for sure." He looked over at Baron, "You've got wheels?"

"I do, and so do you guys, but you're not driving," he declared, "not with those head injuries."

"I'll take one vehicle, and you take the other," Brittany stated.

He looked over at her and then slowly nodded. "Not a bad idea."

"I'm not letting a civilian drive me to the hospital," Anthony snapped. "I might have a head injury, but I can get myself out of here."

It was obvious that he was still pissed and irritated, so she just shrugged. "*Fine*, but we're coming behind you to confirm you make it."

He stared at her for a moment, and his shoulders slumped. "Yeah, that's probably a good idea. Thanks for saving our hides."

With one man on either side of Josh, they made their way to where the vehicles were. The cops now settled in theirs, she walked back to Baron's truck. "I still don't think we should let them drive," she muttered.

"I agree, but what will you do when they are so stubborn? Yet I can't say I blame them or would be any different. And what would you do to stop them? Fight them for the car keys?"

"No." She groaned. "You can't talk sense into men … a lot of times." She waved her hands around, irritated as hell. "I sure can't talk any sense into them right now, not when they're feeling pretty angry over having been taken out like that."

He smiled at her. "It is a bit embarrassing to be found that way," he shared. "For a couple young cops like that, I'm sure this is not something they would want anybody else to see."

"Right," she muttered, "so who gives a crap?"

He just laughed. She got into the vehicle with him, and Kingston got into the back seat. They came up behind the two officers, driving slowly forward. When they got up to the main road, they followed them right through to the hospital.

"I would say that's a sign that they aren't feeling that well," she murmured, as she watched them pull up in front of the emergency entrance.

"Ya think?" Just then, two other cops pulled up behind them.

"Of course they're here now," she grumbled, with an eye roll.

"We don't know where they were before, so remember that."

"Of course." She sighed. "You want me to behave and to keep my mouth shut, but it sure seems like they're never where you need them."

"That's not true either," he pointed out.

"You could just let me grumble for a while."

He burst out laughing and nodded. "That I might do." They were forced to get out and talk to the other officers, who had just arrived.

The story was taken down once and then twice, with parts repeated again for everybody who asked questions, and finally they were told they could leave but needed to stay close—in case they had any more questions.

It took them about an hour answering all the damn questions. By the time she got back into the vehicle, she groaned and hung her head. "I just want to get some sleep now."

He smiled. "Just imagine if you had stayed where you were and hadn't decided to come along with me."

"Yeah, just imagine where we would be," she pointed out.

"Hey, I'm not saying you shouldn't have come," he added. "I am glad to have a level head out there. Yet it would have been nice if you didn't go through all this. It might save you some nightmares."

She smiled and nodded. "I'm not arguing that, for sure," she murmured.

CHAPTER 9

WHEN BRITTANY WOKE up the next morning, she rolled over and stretched and then groaned, as her body screamed at her. She lay here for a few minutes, letting her brain fully wake up. When she remembered, it was almost worse. She stood up slowly, realizing that even though she hadn't been doing a lot of physical work, just the trampling in the darkness back and forth in unsteady debris-filled terrain, plus dealing with the gunman and the emotional stress, had all left an immense soreness inside her.

Yet she got more sleep than Baron did because he was intent on finding a twenty-four hour veterinarian to give Kingston a good once-over. No telling how long that took.

She got up slowly and headed for a shower. It didn't always fix everything, but it sure felt good. By the time she was done and dressed, she wondered how Baron had fared through all this. He'd been the hero picking up and securing everybody, and she hadn't even asked him about the War Dog.

Swearing at that oversight, she quickly sent him a text. **What happened to Kingston overnight?**

In response, she got a short video back of Kingston, stretched out on the bed, snoring, and it showed a strange but intimate shot of Baron still in bed too.

Lucky you, she sent back. **I'm up and sore as hell.**

Go back to bed, he ordered.

She smiled, loving the fact that at least that level of humor and rapport existed between them. But, instead of trying to answer in another long text, she phoned him.

"Good morning," he answered cheerfully.

"How come you're so cheerful?"

"Isn't it enough that I still haven't gotten out of bed?" he asked, with that same dry humor coming through the phone.

She smiled. "Lucky you," she repeated ruefully. "I woke up and decided a hot shower would be required."

"Are you sore?" he asked.

She hesitated and then realized no point in lying and admitted, "Yeah, I am a little bit, though I'm not sure why."

"Did you trip and fall last night? Did the gunman hit you?"

"No, he didn't. I'm glad you found Kingston, so now what? Is the job done?"

"No, not yet. I have to find out where his owners are and what's going on with his housing situation. I have to ensure he gets home to his people." He yawned.

"Look at that," she teased. "Seems you're ready to go back to sleep."

"As much as I would like that," he replied, "it's not an option."

"Oh, why not? What are you up to now?"

"In case you've forgotten, I still need to figure out why those gunmen were up there."

She frowned. "Are you telling me that you won't leave that to the cops?"

"It's not so much that I won't let the cops do their job," he clarified, "but definitely something is off about that whole scenario."

"And *something off* means that you have to look for it?" she asked, staring at the phone.

"Maybe," he muttered. "Again, this is something that I do, so it would be hard for me to just walk away."

"But maybe you need to," she said, alarmed. "Sometimes no good can come from this."

He smiled. "Does that mean you're worried about me?"

"Yes, I am worried about you. I most certainly am. After what we saw down there, it's not awe-inspiring to think that more of this crap may be happening."

"Right, and it's one of the reasons I want to confirm it's all okay."

Something in his tone she didn't quite understand. "You're not telling me something."

"I'm not telling you lots of things," he admitted.

"Well, I guess you need to tell me a few things. For instance, is it dangerous for me now?"

"No," he stated.

She hesitated. "Why not? How can you be so sure? The gunman is on the loose, and he saw me."

"That's very true," he replied thoughtfully, "and we never did find out what they were looking for. We never found his partner either."

"Exactly, so that's why I'm asking if you think I'm in danger."

"I don't think you're particularly in danger," he murmured, "any more than the rest of us, but it is a consideration. If he couldn't get what he wanted from us down there, I don't think he'll bother coming back."

"Maybe," she muttered, as she stared off into the distance. "Still, it's a little unnerving."

"True. It's also one of the reasons we want to bring this

to a conclusion."

She agreed with that but had no idea what she was supposed to do. He was the one with the skill sets in this area, so it only made sense that she should stick with him.

"Do you want to go out for breakfast?" he asked and then laughed. "Unless you've had enough of my company."

"Oh no, that's not it," she said in buoyed spirits, "and it's probably a good idea. That way we can talk about what's next."

"*Uh-oh*, I probably shouldn't have mentioned it then."

"No, you probably shouldn't have," she agreed cheerfully, "but you have, so now I want to know exactly what's going on."

"Nothing's going on," he replied. "I'm just not sure that I'm ready to walk away."

"If you're not, I'm not either. So I guess I'll stick with you."

"This isn't what you do though," he pointed out. "Remember that part. This can be dangerous. This is what I do, but you don't have to be putting yourself in harm's way."

"Maybe not, but remember that part about it's what you *used* to do?" she added.

He laughed. "Ouch. Look. Tell me a good breakfast spot, and I'll meet you there."

She thought about it for a moment and suggested, "How about the inn down on the lake? They do a morning brunch, and I'm hungry."

"Me too, so it's a brunch, *huh*?"

"Yeah, I think it might be a buffet brunch, but I'm not positive."

"I guess we'll find out when we get there. I'll head off and get a shower."

"Good enough," she said, with a smile.

She hopped off the call and looked back at her bedroom. She was too damn tired to make the bed. Yet it was one of those deeply entrenched habits that she'd been brought up. Whether she made her bed or not today, she still needed to pop by to see Grandma and to see if everything was okay over there.

As she approached Camille's, she found her grandma standing in the open doorway, just looking at her. "Is everything okay?" Brittany asked. "I was just heading out to brunch and thought I would pop by."

"Heading to brunch," Grandma repeated shrewdly.

"Yes." Then realized that her grandmother would now have a million and one questions.

"I heard you were out getting in trouble last night."

Stopping in her tracks, she stared at her. "I don't know about getting into trouble," she replied, guarded. "I was certainly out last night and definitely ran into some trouble. How the hell did you hear about it?"

"I heard about it, and that's all you need to know," her grandmother muttered. "I really don't need any of that crap from my house that bad, and you know it."

"I know, but you already lost your house, so you shouldn't have to lose all the important things you care about too."

Her grandmother gave her a warm smile. "That may be," she conceded, eyeing her intently. "But I don't want anything to happen to you," she muttered. "That would be the worst-case scenario."

Touched by her words, Brittany gave her a hug and muttered, "I won't do anything stupid."

"Maybe you won't, but I also heard Baron was involved."

She laughed. "He was involved, but he was also the rescuer in this case."

"Oh? Now that sounds interesting." Grandma gave her a bright smile. "Why don't you come in and tell me more."

"I can't right now," she said, with a chuckle. "I'm heading off to breakfast."

"With Baron?"

"*Yes*," she replied in an exaggerated way, "with Baron."

"Ah, good. That's very good." Grandma waved her off. "Go on now. … You can talk to me afterward."

Smiling, Brittany got back into her car and headed to the brunch spot. She hadn't been here in quite a few years, so she hoped it was still as good as she remembered. As she pulled in the parking lot, she got out and thought about wandering down to the beach area for a little bit, when a dog ran toward her.

When she recognized him, she bent down and called out, "Hey, Kingston. Greetings like that would break a girl's heart." She looked up to see Baron strolling along behind the War Dog.

"How did you get here so fast?" she asked.

"I was closer than you," he explained. "Besides, this guy wanted to get out and run a bit."

"I don't know if Kingston will be allowed in the restaurant." She frowned, as she turned to look for any signs about pets.

"As long as you're okay to sit outside, he is. I already called and checked."

"Oh, that's perfect then," she murmured.

They walked around the restaurant to the big veranda on the back set up for dining. She smiled as she looked around.

"I haven't been here in a very long time."

"I'm pretty impressed so far, and the food smells and looks great," he noted. "Or I could just be very hungry."

"Or both," she added pointedly, as she smiled at him. Regardless, by the time they sat down and ordered coffee, Kingston had stretched out on the patio beside her, more than ready to just crash and relax.

"He's really calm and chill, isn't he?" she noted, as she got up and walked over to the buffet with Baron.

"Absolutely, and I'm really happy to see his training kept him on his toes as well. He seems really solid."

"You sound as if you don't really want to hand him over."

"I'm not sure I do. If I had a reason or an opportunity to keep him, I probably would," he shared, with a smile. "He's a good dog, and he listens really well. His training is still pretty-much intact. He could be a hell of a search and rescue animal."

She studied him and then nodded, "I never did ask what you do."

"Right now, I don't do much of anything," he stated. "I was still making plans for when I was back on my feet."

"Do you not consider yourself back on your feet now?" she asked.

"Yes and no, but I can't say I thought it would all happen that fast."

"Ah, now that I can believe. Life has a way of happening when we're not looking."

He grinned at her. "I think I've heard that phrase a time or two."

"Yeah, it's a staple in this part of the world at least. It was one of my mom's favorite phrases."

"Do you miss her?"

She hesitated and then shrugged. "Not my mother so much," she admitted, feeling a bit sheepish. "I know that sounds terrible, but it was a rough life with her around. My grandma is the one who's always been there for me," she explained. "So, if anything happens to her, it would hurt badly, and, in the meantime, I'm really hoping she can live the life she deserves."

"Of course, and I'm sorry. We always seem to think that childhood is this big happy picture-perfect scenario, but so often it isn't that way at all."

"No, all too often it isn't. Yet, for me, it ended up in a great way because I do have my grandma. A lot of kids out there didn't have anyone to pick up the slack."

"Which is also why you feel guilty about not rushing to pick up the slack with your grandma."

"Exactly," she stated. "It's not easy to reconcile the reality that I really don't want to do it."

"Caretaking is not an easy job. It takes a special person to handle that job, day in and day out. And you would need some relief help because it's hard on full-time caretakers. Regardless, I'm sure your grandmother is totally okay with staying at your place—or someplace close to you."

"Well, I don't know about that because it's a conversation that still needs to happen."

He smiled. "I think you're worrying too much."

"Maybe, I don't know. I just want to ensure that she's happy and that I can have something of a life too. I love her dearly, and I feel terrible that I don't necessarily want to take over 100 percent of her care."

"Again, that's one of the reasons why you need to talk to her because she might have other ideas anyway. Taking over her care also sounds very much as if she would be limited, and that may not be what she wants either."

"It's absolutely not what she wants," Brittany declared, with a knowing smile. "She loves her independence and having her own home."

"That's good to hear, so maybe you could set up some arrangement where she can have that again."

"I don't know if we can salvage her house. Even if insurance did cover all the damage, it won't be an easy thing to hire contractors and get the work done. Plus it always takes longer to do these repairs than is first estimated. The wait can be stressful enough."

"I think your grandmother is probably a whole lot more resilient than you give her credit for. A lot of times the older generation manages to snap back, while the rest of us are all still sitting around, stunned, wondering what happened."

She smiled. "I agree with you there," she muttered.

Kingston kept impressing her the entire time. He sat through lunch, didn't beg in any way, and, when the server came out and asked if he could have a little bit of bacon, he didn't appear to care either way. But when he was signaled that it was okay to eat it, he scooped it up, then looked at them with such appreciation and joy that Brittany had to smile. "I don't think I've ever seen such a well-trained dog," she murmured. "He's really wonderful."

Baron smiled at her and then said, "And Kingston's got you completely buffaloed."

She burst out laughing and agreed. "You're right, and he can keep me buffaloed too, if this is the behavior he puts on. No wonder people like these dogs so much."

"Not to mention that they're really good for protection, if needed."

"Yet what happened to the man who had him?"

"My brother had Kingston, until he was in the hospital, and somebody was supposed to look after this guy in the interim. After the hurricane hit, I'm not sure what happened. The dogsitter didn't figure Kingston was worth looking after, or he figured the dog would be better off on his own, or some other life crisis happened." Baron waved his hands. "We can't really judge until we know."

"And it's so easy to judge, isn't it?" she muttered, with a smile. "It's so easy to just assume that whoever it was just bailed on the dog."

"Exactly, but we don't know that, so, until we have more information, we'll hold off on judgment until we see."

She smiled at him. "Why don't you set up rescue dog training? You seem to understand and to handle them pretty well."

"In this case, Kingston's pretty easy to handle because he's already been well-trained," he noted. "I would just need to pick up the training and keep it going."

"That's certainly an option. You would have a good base here."

"I don't know."

"Well, your brother built a community for himself here just dealing with rescuing dogs," she pointed out. "So you can do something related to the dogs as well."

He nodded. "I've certainly thought about it, and my brother was always trying to coerce me to move back here. Right now I've been feeling an awful lot of regret that I didn't."

"Of course you are. That's human nature in a situation like this," she replied. "Yet *there is a time for everything*, and, if it wasn't the time for it, then maybe it's a better time now."

He looked over at her and nodded. "We'll see."

"Which I'll take as a request to butt out. I get it," she said, as she burst out laughing at the surprised look on his face.

"That's not what I meant," he protested. "It really is a case of *we'll see* more than anything else. I was just getting cleared to return to work, but I'm not going back into the military. So I'm not sure what my future work will look like."

"Yet you get a pension, and you don't have to work like the rest of us, or is that not right?"

"I'll get a pension, but it won't be enough to take care of everything I'll need for the rest of my life," he shared. "So, no, I definitely need to find an occupation, maybe a niche of my own to keep the lights on." He studied her for a long moment and added, "I really like the idea of search and rescue and maybe a shelter home."

Again she noticed that infectious grin spread across his face. That grin was lit, and she had to admit she would do an awful lot to keep it coming. He rarely seemed to smile at all yesterday, but then he was still only beginning to deal with the shock and the loss of his brother's death. "I am so sorry about Brad," she said. "Your brother was a special man. Yet he wasn't married, was he?"

Baron shook his head. "He did once, but it was a brief marriage. She lied to him about being pregnant, so he was gun-shy after that. Plus, with his heart condition, he didn't want to get too attached and then end up leaving somebody behind with a family he couldn't look after."

"And yet he could have had many years to bring joy to somebody's life," she pointed out.

"I think he was happy the way he was, and he figured, if he found the right woman, then good. If not, well, it wasn't meant to be."

She wondered about that. "Just with the little bit that I knew of him, he probably would have remained single."

"Maybe, but he wasn't unhappy by any means," Baron stated. "Not everybody has to be married in order to be happy."

She nodded. "It's usually me saying that to people," she noted, with a laugh, "so hearing it come out of your mouth just shows me how far I've fallen." He raised an eyebrow, and she explained. "After a decent amount of time had passed after my breakup at the altar, a lot of people told me that I needed to just get out there and to keep trying to find the right person. I kept telling them that I didn't want to be married or connected to somebody else in order to be happy, but nobody believed me."

He smiled. "That's the problem with being single in an insensitive world," he explained. "Everybody thinks you can't be happy unless you're paired up. Then, when you are paired up, you're not allowed to be unhappy because then you're automatically part of the world that's about to get divorced."

"I never thought of it that way," she muttered, shaking her head. "Yet you're right. It's not easy being the odd man out, is it?"

"No, it sure isn't."

She tilted her head and asked, "What about you?"

"Never been married, though I was in a serious relationship before my accident," he shared. "I thought we were heading there, but she was against my going back into the military, worried that I would end up the way I am, and that's not the life she wanted." He looked down at his leg and shrugged. "Better to have found out before, instead of coming back like this, only to find out she wouldn't be there for me," he stated, with a crooked smile. "We never really know what people are truly like, not until we get into a situation such as this. So I'm glad she was upfront and honest about it."

"Still, I can't imagine saying that to somebody," Brittany declared. "I thought, when you loved somebody, you loved them regardless, and the rest didn't matter."

"Apparently not," he quipped, "because her love required me to be whole, and, if I were to come back broken, … it was on me, and she wasn't interested."

"Wow," she muttered, staring at him. "That must have hurt."

He laughed. "It did, but it was a long time ago, and it's all good now."

"Is it though?"

"Absolutely." He shot her a glance. "No point hanging on to that stuff, and at least she was honest about it. I can appreciate honesty." Standing up, he added, "I'm going back for seconds."

She laughed as she watched him head off to the buffet to get more food. It was a joy to see somebody with an appetite. So often these days everybody—at least the women in her age group—were all watching what they ate and, therefore, never ate much at all.

It was frustrating because Brittany had a healthy appetite now, even though most people still looked at her sideways when she ate. She couldn't ever shake that persona of who she used to be, no matter how much she tried. For Baron, that had to be part of it too. There would always be people who saw him in the physical condition he was in, not understanding that it really wouldn't have too much of an impact on him.

When he returned with a full plate, she looked at it. "Okay, so round two is one thing, but, wow, that's a lot of food."

"It is, but this way I don't have to worry about trying to find more food, when I'm heading out again."

She stopped and looked at him with exasperation. "So, you really are going back out?"

"Of course I am," he confirmed agreeably, "but this time I'm taking Kingston with me."

"Oh, that's a really good idea," she noted. "I didn't think about that. Plus you still have to track down his owner."

"Badger is doing that," he relayed, with a shrug, "but I figured Kingston could use the exercise and the training, so I might as well make good use of his skills while we're there."

She felt an odd unease about his going back out alone, but, with Kingston by his side, maybe it was okay.

He smiled at her. "He'll be extra protection too. You know that, right?"

"How did you know what I was thinking? Are you a mind reader now too?"

In the process of taking a bite, he burst out laughing, then ended up having a coughing fit, bringing extra attention their way. He shook his head. "No, but, in this case, it was obvious."

She glared at him. "It was not."

"It was."

As they wrangled good-naturedly, the waitress came over and filled up their coffee. "You guys must have known each other for a long time," she said, "because, wow, you're having way-too-much fun," And, wearing a big grin, she disappeared.

Brittany looked over at him. "I guess that's what most people would think, wouldn't they?"

"Doesn't matter what they think," he said easily. "I'm well past the stage of giving a crap. Aren't you?"

She thought about it and nodded. "I've lived under the eagle eyes of this town for a very long time," she muttered. "So, yeah, I'm more than happy to ditch that constant worrying about people judging me."

"As soon as you started eating and dealing with some of your earlier issues," he began, "that should have fallen by the wayside itself. Still, when you live in a small town like this, it never really goes away. Everybody is always worrying and watching, making sure that you're okay."

"Isn't that the truth?"

"On the other hand, maybe it's a good thing, since it shows that the town is full of heart."

She looked at him and smiled. "Honestly, I think it is full of heart. It's just not always the easiest town to live in."

"No, I can't imagine that it would be." He leaned closer to her and whispered, "So, as soon as we're done here, I'm heading back into that area. What will you do?"

She nodded. "Do you want company?" When he hesitated, she raised her hands. "I know. I know. You want to go alone. I get it."

"I do want to go alone, though it's not necessarily the smartest thing to do. But, if you'll go up that way behind me, even to poke around at your grandma's place, I would rather you not be up there alone."

She studied him and started to laugh and laugh. "Aha. So, that's the way to let me come with you. I just have to let you think I'll go anyway." That lopsided grin slipped onto his face, melting her heart a little bit more.

"Maybe," he said, with a self-conscious shrug. "I do need to keep you safe."

"Didn't you just tell me that it was safe?"

"Yeah, and I think it is. I don't think that'll be the issue, but what I don't know is whether our gunmen will continue searching for whatever it is they need."

"It's daylight now, and that might affect their decision-making too," she noted.

"I suggest we both go."

"Since you're taking Kingston, why don't we trample around on our own down there? Then, if you think it's safe, I can stay around my grandma's house and do some work and look for stuff for her."

"I agree. Let's go take a look. Then, depending on how everything feels, maybe you can continue doing your thing, while I continue on mine."

"Done." She raised her hand, and the waitress came over with their bill. They paid at the table, leaving a generous tip, and, as they walked out, she asked him, "I have my wheels here. What do you want to do about that?"

He nodded. "How about I just follow you back to your place, and we'll go from there."

And that's what they did. By the time she parked in her driveway, then slipped over to his truck, she noted, "I forgot you even knew where I lived."

He looked at her and laughed. "I guess you were so tired last night that you don't remember my following you home?"

"It did take a minute this morning, as I was sitting there thinking about it," she admitted, "and, yeah, that's how tired

I was. I don't want to be that tired and stressed out again."

"Hopefully not," he agreed, with a smile. "I was thinking that maybe we could do dinner Friday."

"Oh, lovely. You have something in mind?"

He nodded. "Some bake thing is going on, isn't there?"

"You mean, the seafood bake?" She stared at him. "I had forgotten about that, but, yes, you're right." She pulled out her phone and checked the calendar. "I think it is Friday night. Good for you."

He laughed. "Not really, my mother mentioned it."

"Will you take her?"

"She doesn't like seafood," he noted, with a smile, "so that would be a waste, but I did tell her that I would consider going." He glanced over at her. "I didn't really want to go alone."

"I get it. I wouldn't want to either."

"Good, in that case, we can be each other's backup. If that's good with you?"

She burst out laughing. "Backup? I would rather just call it a date."

He looked over at her, raised an eyebrow, and laughed. "That's great with me. Absolutely, if it's okay with you."

She gave him a bright smile. "Yeah, it's fine. Besides, it will give everybody a chance to see that I'm normal again."

"Do you really think they still need to see that?"

"I don't know, but sometimes, yeah. Sometimes it feels like they still haven't seen that I'm okay."

"Maybe you just haven't put yourself out there enough to be seen that much."

"Maybe." She shrugged. "It's not really my scene. I would just as soon forget that part of my life."

"I agree with you totally. So, we'll go to the seafood

bake, and you'll eat up a storm. They'll be amazed at your appetite and wonder how on earth anybody could afford to feed you now."

She burst out laughing, and their banter continued, as they headed back to the area of her grandmother's house. Seeing it in the daylight again was sobering, and she sighed heavily as they came up on it.

"Did you contact the insurance company?"

"My grandma was trying to do that when I left, and Camille was helping her," she muttered, "but it's not easy right now, after the hurricane affected so many. So trying to get anybody on the phone is one big hurdle. Then trying to get the insurance adjuster to move quickly isn't easy either, not in this situation."

"Not to mention there has to be building materials, tradesmen, architects, and all kinds of other things around here to make it all happen," he murmured, "and that'll be in short supply."

"Right, and all these things that should make life easy— because we paid for them ages ago—tend to go out the window as soon as a disaster hits."

"Insurance isn't all bad," he said, "and, in a case like this, it could turn out to be a godsend."

"Maybe, but it's also quite possible that they'll end up fighting it." When he looked at her, she shrugged. "That's what my grandma seems to think."

"But, if she had insurance, she had coverage for exactly this kind of event."

"Yes, I know, but she doesn't have the same faith."

"Let's hope this is the instance that restores it then," he said. "An awful lot of people are out there who would need help right now, so the insurance companies will have a hard time working their way out from under it."

"But you know how it is. … If they can get out of paying something, they will."

He smiled. "I'm not saying that they won't try. I'm just saying that you will have other resources available to you to help fight them, if that should be an issue."

"I still think you have a very Pollyanna attitude," she said, with a smile.

He glared at her in horror. "That sounds absolutely horrific."

She chuckled. "I don't think so. It's very typical of life. I don't want to be disappointed."

"Maybe," he admitted, "but certainly an awful lot is going on in this world that we can't ever really sort out, and it would be nice to think we had backup when needed."

"I would like to think so, but …"

"And here we are back to that *needing more faith* discussion," he pointed out.

"For somebody who's been through as much as you have, you seem an awful lot more optimistic than I am."

He shrugged. "I've also come out on the other side, and I have to admit being on this side is a whole lot easier than being where I was. I'm just grateful I'm not there anymore."

"Oh, I like that too," she agreed, with a nod. "We do get stuck in our own heads, don't we?"

"We absolutely do, and it's one of the loneliest places you can ever be," he stated, with a look in her direction, "as you well know."

She nodded slowly. "You're very perceptive."

"Sometimes, but it's mostly just the facts of life. I may have seen a little more than I would have liked to have seen of life," he noted, with a chuckle. At that, Kingston barked from the back seat. He looked over at him. "You doing okay there, buddy?"

He barked several more times as they passed a Starbucks. "What is it, buddy?" Kingston was barking and barking and barking. Baron glanced over at her and raised one eyebrow.

She shrugged. "I don't have a clue. Could he recognize something here?"

"It depends on whether he was addicted to pup cups," he suggested, with a groan. He flashed a grin her way and asked, "How about a coffee?"

"A coffee or a pup cup?" she asked suspiciously.

He pulled into the drive-through. As he reached the front, the window opened, and the woman standing there cried out, "It's Kingston."

He sighed. "I'm looking after him for a little while, but he barked as we came past, and I was afraid he was addicted to pup cups."

"Oh, he totally is, but he's also a big brave boy," she replied, "and we give it to him for free." Then she handed over this pup cup, full of whipping cream. Kingston almost howled in delight. The barista grinned. "You guys want a coffee or just the pup cup for him?"

Feeling terrible, he looked over at Brittany, and she nodded. "Two coffees to go, please. Also can you tell me who brought Kingston here for his treats? I'm trying to locate his owner."

The barista just frowned. "Funny, I don't know his name. We all go crazy over Kingston, yet I never thought to ask the man for his name too."

"Can you describe him?" Baron asked.

"He was an older man, but that's about all I remember. Sorry."

"Any memory of the vehicle he drove?"

She winced. "Not really. Things get a little hectic around here most days. However, we do love to interact with the animals as they come through."

Baron nodded. "Understood."

With Kingston lapping up the pup cup and making a mess of whipped cream everywhere, causing everybody to laugh, they finally received two cups of coffee to go. As he drove away, he looked over at Brittany and asked, "So, what do you think?"

She snorted. "That dog is deadly. Deadly and well-loved apparently, and that's something you and Badger have to figure out," she said, raising her shoulders in a shrug, "because somebody might want him back."

"If he wants him back, he gets him back," Baron stated instantly. "I would never do that to anybody, particularly another veteran."

"Oh, right, I never even think of you in that capacity."

"Don't start now," he added, with a smile. "It's not always the easiest label for any of us to wear."

"Ah, I'm not big on labels either," she muttered. "They tend to be the wrong ones and the kind you don't like to hear and see. Or, worse, they limit us. I've read where retired people have a hard time once that label is gone when their job is done. If we are doing any labeling, then we all should have multiple labels to counteract being stuck with just one."

"Exactly, so we're not into adopting a single label."

"Especially not any negative ones," she added.

And, with that, he headed back toward their destination, driving past her grandmother's house once again. This time he pulled off to the side of the road to have a look around the general area.

He noted, "It looks pretty empty, and we didn't see anybody on the way in."

"I know. The other day quite a few people were trying to salvage stuff, but it looks as if nobody's really coming back." When he hesitated, she waved him off. "I'm fine to stay here. So you go do your thing, and then you can come back for me."

"Okay. You've got my phone number, right?"

"I've got your phone number, and everything's fine." She exited his truck and smiled at him, as he drove away, Kingston now in the front seat as if he belonged there.

"Kingston, you are one crazy dude," she muttered, as he barked at her as a way of saying goodbye. But he was happy and healthy, and he appeared to be fairly well adjusted to life, so it was great that it was going so well.

She headed around to the back of her grandmother's house, once again looking for bits and pieces of her grandma's life that were worth salvaging. Some more of the house had fallen down overnight, which surprised her. She stopped and stared at it, realizing just how much damage there still was and could be to this place.

It was heartbreaking to see, and yet the sooner she adapted to it, the better it would be. Her grandma would adjust, but it would also take a bit of time. As Brittany walked around the outside of the house, where the most things had collected, she thought she saw something sticking out of the ground, partially covered by other debris. Bending down, she picked it up and realized it was a piece of her grandma's jewelry box, and, with that, the hunt was on.

BARON DROVE DOWN to where they'd picked up the officers last night, stopping on the road several times to study the layout. It was desolate, abandoned, and looked horrific in the daylight. He was sure that, for many people, this was one of the most devastating sights they would ever see in their life. The fact that it was their own property and possessions, their lives, histories, and memories, made it just that much harder for them.

His brother's house was farther down, and he knew the amount of damage, although minor, still hurt. At least it was easily fixable. Baron had been giving serious thought as to whether he could rebuild rather than completely let it go. The building was mostly sound still, and that was something he needed to talk to the insurance company about.

He fully expected to get his brother's house back up and running in no time. The question was, did he want to move into it, or would stepping into his brother's shoes be too much?

It felt wrong in so many ways.

Baron had told his brother several times that Brad wasn't living life to the fullest because he was so afraid that it would end prematurely, which it had. Brad used to tell Baron basically the same thing. That Baron had gone off to war to serve his country, but when was that service over? And when did the rest of the family count?

The brothers had taken a position where they were both right, and they were both wrong. If Baron could have gone back and made some changes, he would have done so to spend more time with Brad.

Even as he thought about his mother, and the years that she was now facing without his brother, Baron knew how hard that would be for her. It's not that Baron wasn't her favorite son, but he just wasn't Brad, and that was the hardest part to ignore.

Nobody could ever be Brad.

Brad was special, and being special also presented a challenge. He'd had his own problems, but he'd always been there for everybody. No reason to consider that there might have been something untoward about his death, except that something about it just didn't ring true to Baron. When that happened, Baron usually hounded that thought, until he figured out what was wrong—which was why he was out here right now.

Brad had had a heart attack, which was something that wasn't totally unexpected, considering his condition, but that also made it much more convenient for somebody to take him out. Plus the heart diagnosis could easily disguise or preclude any real determination of his death. If somebody had been involved in ending Brad's life, Baron could never make peace with the unknown.

He couldn't stop thinking that maybe he was just harboring some fantasy. Did Baron consider something happening to his brother as a better alternative than Brad just having had a heart attack and sending the truck into the water, going out the way he'd always lived? Brad had been peaceful in life and now peaceful in death.

And yet every time Baron thought about the truck left in the aftermath, his brother dead inside, it just didn't seem real. If Brad could have, his brother would definitely have delivered those dogs. It would have meant the world to Brad. Since he couldn't, then what would Baron do now, and what could he do? The animals had been in the back of the vehicle, and most of them had been rescued. He didn't even know if any others were still missing.

He continued to drive about the neighborhood, then turned and looked at Kingston and asked, "Are you still hiding something, buddy?"

Kingston looked at him and barked.

Baron pulled off to the side of the road, where he wanted to check the area near the one house that apparently had the notorious Galloway gang crime ring involved. As soon as he opened the truck door, Kingston jumped out and bolted.

Swearing that he hadn't thought to put a lead on the War Dog, Baron called out for Kingston, but the dog was gone. He stared after him, wondering what the hell was so important that the War Dog had disappeared so quickly. But he didn't have much of a choice, since the dog was his responsibility. And, with that, he clambered after him.

CHAPTER 10

BRITTANY SPENT SEVERAL hours puttering around the debris gathered at her grandma's house. She'd managed to fill a couple boxes with things she thought her grandmother would like and had called her a few times to ask her about several items. It would all be cleaned up one way or another, but these were things that were really special and would make it back to her grandmother, not into the bucket of whatever excavator came through here to scoop up the remnants of the lives torn apart all around her.

Her grandmother had okayed everything that Brittany had collected so far, with another warning about being careful. She'd smiled at that. Hopefully her grandmother didn't know all the details about last night because there would be hell to pay. It would really upset Grandma if she thought that her granddaughter was really in danger from armed looters and the like.

Almost anybody would say being at the blunt end of a gun was putting herself in danger. Not that Brittany had done it on purpose by any means. Again that wouldn't make a damn bit of difference to her grandma. She was alone, and the last thing she wanted was to lose the only other family member in her life. At the end of the day, things were just things, and Brittany understood that.

She struggled herself, as she wandered through the mess,

deciding what her options were and what more she should do about rescuing the few items she would love to save for Grandma. Brittany definitely should take her grandmother into her home, which she would, and that was fine. She just needed a little bit of time to get used to the concept. Convincing her grandmother wouldn't be the easiest process either, but, if that's what needed to happen, well, that was fine too. Her grandmother had always been there for her. Thinking back to her conversation with Baron about insurance, she wondered if her grandmother was thinking about trying to get her own house back.

Britany sighed. That was a discussion they must have somewhat soon. Still Brittany dreaded it. Yet this change had been thrust upon her and her grandmother.

As Brittany wandered around, she kept looking at her watch, wondering how long Baron would be. She hadn't considered that, when she was ready to leave, she didn't have any transportation, not until Baron finished with his search.

Swearing at that oversight, she sent him a text, asking for a time frame. When no answer came, she stared down at her phone, then looked off into the distance, worried. If he hadn't answered by now, what was going on that was stopping him?

That was something she didn't even want to consider. Yet now that she hadn't gotten a response from him, it was all she could consider.

She put her salvaged items off to the side and started the short walk down the road. She came to the now-familiar stretch fairly quickly but still saw no sign of Baron. As she kept walking, she continued sending him texts, hoping he would answer, and she hadn't gone too much farther when she heard a bark.

Kingston.

She smiled, then picked up the pace, wondering whether Kingston was once again at work or something else was going on. Moments later she heard another bark.

She froze, trying to determine if it was another dog or if that had really been Kingston's bark. Going a little bit slower, she felt a bit more uncertain about what she was walking into. Reeling, as memories from the previous night inundated her, she came up to another house, looking around for any sign of Kingston.

As she watched, something darted across her path, and it was him. She smiled and called out to him. He came barreling toward her, jumped up, and gave her the greeting that she had been hoping for.

With her arms wrapped around him, she whispered, "Where's Baron? Good boy, … show me Baron." As soon as she gave him a little bit of wiggle room, Kingston was off and running again.

"Shit," she muttered in a panic, knowing that she couldn't keep up with him.

Would he care? Would he slow down long enough for her to catch up, or was she expected to maintain the same grueling pace?

She shook her head at that, knowing she wasn't in that kind of shape. She managed to keep him in sight, but only because he stopped several times to look back at her, giving her a look that seemed to say, *Hey, what's taking you so long?*

By the time she finally caught up to the War Dog, she stopped because he hadn't brought her to Baron. He had brought her to a female dog, who was curled up in a box, and a liter of newborn puppies were beside her.

"Wow, wow, wow," she exclaimed. As she bent down

over the dog. Kingston jumped up beside her and nudged her away ever-so-slightly, not so much as a warning but more of a guideline on being careful.

She smiled at him. "I don't think they're your babies, buddy. I have a hunch that ability had been taken away from you a long time ago." Then she looked over at the female. "I also don't know if she's hurt."

Brittany approached, talking to the other dog, whose tail wagged weakly. "Yeah, we need to get you out of here too, sweetheart. Are you one of the dogs that went missing?" It would make sense in a way, especially if they were stuck for too long. If Kingston had managed to get out, then maybe this mama dog had followed him, needing a place to have her puppies. That could hold her for so long, but maybe it hadn't been quite long enough.

She stood and asked Kingston, "Now where's Baron?"

He barked several more times and then took off.

She groaned. "Okay, now hang on a minute. I can't just keep chasing you around this damn mess, particularly when something could trip me up and could break my neck with each step I take." With a promise to the mama dog and all her snoozing puppies, Brittany headed off again, chasing Kingston. The walking was heavy going.

Another fifteen to twenty minutes later, all of a sudden, his barking stopped. She frowned as she crept forward once again, now feeling completely ill at ease over whatever was going on here.

The fact that Kingston had been barking, almost as a guiding light for her to follow and to get somewhere, but then stopped so abruptly, made her incredibly uneasy. She didn't have a specific reason to be worried, except for everything that had happened yesterday evening and the fact that Baron hadn't responded to her texts. She crept forward slowly now, not hearing Kingston anymore. As she waited between steps, she thought she heard a voice, then a yelp, and the voice again. Then a much harsher yelp and a much harsher voice.

Not sure what was going on, she edged forward. As she crept around part of a still-standing structure that looked to be an old shed, she turned to see Kingston, a rope partially around his neck. He wasn't fighting it, but he looked very confused. Beside him was a man she didn't recognize, but something about him she instinctively didn't like. Maybe it was the fact that he was yelling at Kingston now.

"You stupid dog, why do you keep coming around here? You'll get me in trouble."

She looked around, wondering what had happened to Baron. He was now uppermost in her mind. She didn't think the rope around Kingston's neck would hold him. She frowned as she considered that. Then, off to the side, came a loud noise, obnoxiously loud, as if something fell to the ground, maybe part of somebody's roof. The man was startled, and Kingston jumped free and took off running. She sighed as she saw that because the chances of her getting close to the War Dog now weren't good.

If he couldn't lead her to Baron, what was she supposed to do?

The stranger stood there, glaring off in the distance. "You stupid fucking dog, don't come back again. If you do and if you bring somebody with you, you can bet I'll pop you one."

Hearing that, she sank back ever-so-slightly, wondering just what was going on here. She looked around, trying to sort out what part of the neighborhood she was in. It shouldn't have been hard to determine, but, with all the landmarks down due to the hurricane, and the roads hardly passable, she was definitely turned around.

When she stopped next, she noted she was close to where Brad's house was, which meant it was also close to the spooky Gorman house. It had been called the spooky house since she was a kid. She had never really thought anything about it until now, as she realized that this angry guy was near the spooky house. She wondered if he had any right to be there.

She supposedly had no right to be at her grandmother's place, and she wasn't listening to the warnings to avoid this area, so she could hardly blame anybody else who owned property here either.

She took a good look at the angry man's face and then slowly retreated. As she stepped back a little bit more, she stepped on Kingston's paw, getting a yelp. Immediately the angry man charged in her direction. She bolted around several more piles of debris, trying to hide, as he continued to yell at the dog.

"What the hell is your problem? Either get over here or get lost. Don't keep hanging around here. I've got shit to do, and you're in my way."

She wasn't sure what he was looking to do, but absolutely nothing was friendly about him, and she didn't recognize him as being from the area at all. She didn't live too far away, but she was just far enough removed that she didn't know everyone who lived here. Still, she did know a lot of them.

She wanted to ask him questions, to pin him down, and to see who he was, but he seemed dangerous, and he definitely was pissed. The last thing she wanted was a confrontation with somebody who was out of sorts with his life, and this guy seemed to be out of sorts with everything. Then it occurred to her that he could also be the missing partner from last night. She had no way of knowing whether he was or not.

Following Kingston again, she tried to stay on ground that didn't make any noise, but it was damn hard. Everything creaked and groaned right now, and shit kept falling down, making it damn hard to stay quiet. As she came around another weird structure that was still standing, she came face-to-face with the stranger.

He looked at her and glared.

She glared right back. "Have you seen my dog?"

His eyebrows shot up. "You're looking for that mutt?" he asked. "He's been a pain in my ass."

"Where is he?" she asked, looking around frantically. All she wanted to do was get away, but she also needed a good excuse for being here, and Kingston had provided her one.

"He's here. Somewhere around here anyway, and, every time I turn around, he's in my way."

She shrugged. "He's probably just trying to help."

"He can help by getting the hell out of my life," he snapped, glaring at her, "and you better get the hell out of here too."

She stiffened and replied, "Nobody's even supposed to be here."

"Yeah? Well, that's nice, lady," he replied, a sneer on his face. "So what are you doing here then?"

"Looking for my dog," she repeated.

He rolled his eyes. "You should just shoot that thing."

"That's totally inappropriate. How could you even say that?" she asked, as she turned around to leave. "What are you even doing here?"

"I have my house here. What are you doing here?"

She kept walking away, her back stiff, tingles running up and down her spine, as she worried about the idea of his coming after her. "I'm looking for my dog. I already told you that."

"Yeah, … well, don't bother coming back around here," he ordered. "No dog is here, and I don't give a shit if one is."

She shook her head and glared at him. "Whatever." And, with that, she picked up her pace and raced away. Only after a few minutes, she turned around to see that hateful man running right behind her.

BARON SAT UP slowly, rubbing his head. He wasn't sure what the hell had happened, but he'd been walking through the area, when the next thing he remembered was seeing stars. When he woke up, he was on his side. All sorts of debris surrounded him, all potential weapons to knock him out.

His head pounded. He slowly got up and heard Kingston barking in the distance. He let out a sharp whistle, but then came silence. Just silence, which was odd.

Maybe the War Dog was coming anyway.

He slowly walked to one of the few utility poles still standing in the area and leaned up against it. He reached up a hand to lightly brush his head, checking for soreness, for blood, as he tried to figure out how long he'd been out. He checked his watch and saw all of the texts from Brittany.

He sent one back. **I'm fine.** Of course he wasn't fine, but he would be. He couldn't tell her that his head was mush.

When she came around the corner of a nearby building, running as fast as she could, while looking behind her, obviously in a panic, he forgot about his headache. Reaching out, he snagged her into his arms and pulled her up behind him. She screamed, but, when she saw who it was, she threw herself into his arms. Unsteady, it almost toppled him to the ground.

"He's following me," she muttered, trying to catch her breath.

He braced himself for whomever was about to come around the corner, only nothing happened. He looked down at her, and she remained frantic.

"He was following me right up to a few minutes ago," she whispered, her hands trembling in a complete panic.

He nodded. "Let me take a look." He peered around the area but saw nothing. He heard footsteps stomping away though. "Seems he's leaving."

"Where were you?" she asked. "I kept texting you, but you didn't answer." He winced, and she noticed the blood on his forehead. "What happened? Oh my God, your head is a mess."

"I'm not sure what happened," he admitted, looking around the place. "Honestly I don't know whether I got hit by someone or something just came down on top of me," he muttered. "At the moment, I've got a doozy of a headache."

She sighed. "That's why you shouldn't be here alone."

He gave her a crooked smile and replied, "Yes, *Mom*."

She rolled her eyes. "The last thing I am feeling is motherly toward you," she declared, with a snap. "Fatherly, maybe, … in the sense that I might smack you for it, but I understand that whole *need to do things* concept. But when I texted you, and you weren't answering, I came looking. Thankfully I ran into Kingston, who ran ahead, and led me to a mama dog and her puppies. We have to go get them, Baron. Then when I saw Kingston next, this really strange man had a rope around Kingston's neck. The man was angry and yelling at Kingston."

"Interesting. So obviously Kingston got free."

"He did, and we left together in a hurry. When I turned to check, the guy was running behind me and catching up. That's when I lost track of Kingston, but I sped up and came around the corner here, where I barreled right into you."

"Well, it's a good thing you did because it was one thing for our angry guy to attack a solo female but quite another to consider coming up against two people."

She nodded. "And yet if he finds out that you're hurt …"

"I'm fine," he repeated firmly.

She rolled her eyes. "Yeah, of course you're fine." She sighed, quiet for a moment. "You do realize how irritating that is?"

"I do," he stated, with a quiet chuckle, "but honestly I feel pretty good. It knocked me out but no permanent damage. I'm just fine."

"If you were knocked out in any way shape or form, you should go to the hospital to get checked out." He now rolled his eyes at her. "You yourself said that very same thing to the officers last night."

"I know, and I did say that," he agreed, raising a hand in defense.

"You're just as stubborn as they were."

He grinned. "I won't say that I'm not, yet I would be very grateful if the headache would stop."

"Sure, but it won't," she stated pointedly. "You've been knocked out, so now your body's got to be screaming for a chance to heal. We need to go."

He nodded. "I think that would be best for right now."

As he turned and led her back toward the truck, she shook her head. "Hell, I totally forgot. Turn around, we're going this way."

He followed her lead, realizing just how much his head was off-kilter, also that his sense of direction was not quite right. "I don't want to leave without Kingston."

"Then call him," she suggested. "Now that we have the truck here, I don't know if this angry guy is likely to come after us or not."

"He also needs a reason to come after us," he pointed out.

"Sure, but I don't think this guy gives a crap about a reason," she muttered. "He's scary. I did wonder if he was the missing partner our gunman from last night was looking for."

Baron nodded. "Could be. So you didn't recognize him at all?"

"Nope. Not that I know every neighbor, but this guy was a complete stranger to me."

Baron then let out a long, sharp whistle.

"Wow," she said, "I wish I could do that."

"I can teach you," he volunteered.

"I don't think it's that easy," she muttered. "I've never been very good at whistling."

He smiled and shook his head. "You can't give up before you've even tried, but we'll save it for another day." He heard barking in the distance, and he whistled again, the same high-pitched sound.

"Don't tell me that you worked with K9 dogs when you were in the military."

He smiled. "Sometimes, yeah. I sure did."

"See? Just like I told you before. Now that you're out of the military, you should just keep working with the dogs. They need somebody who understands them."

"That's my intent, but we'll see," he replied.

She looked like she would pound the point a little more, but just then Kingston flew around the corner and barreled right into them, as the dog pounced on Baron, he went down hard. The War Dog was obviously ecstatic to see him. "Well, look at that," she muttered, from the sideline. "You should ask to keep him."

"Somebody else has a prior claim, remember? I won't even have a choice in the matter, unless something has changed."

"Right, but if you do have a choice in the matter?"

"Look who we have here," snapped a man from behind them.

She stiffened, then turned around.

Baron looked up to see a stranger staring at them. "Hey," he greeted him in an unnervingly friendly tone. "Glad to see he is out making friends."

"This is your dog?" the angry man asked. Baron nodded, and the guy snorted. "That thing is a piece of shit, and it's always in my face, always disturbing me, always causing trouble," he complained. "So, if it's your dog, just keep it the hell away from me, or I'll shoot it."

At the sound of the angry man's tone, Kingston turned and growled softly, coming from deep in his throat.

"Yeah, you," the angry man snarled at him, "Keep that piece of shit away from me. Where do you live anyway?" he asked, as Baron stood up.

"Where do you live?" Baron asked.

"None of your fucking business."

"Yet it is part of my fucking business, as I'm part of the crew who keeps an eye on this area. You give me an address where you live, so I can check that out, or else I'll be bringing in the cops."

Instantly the silence around them grew thick and ugly. The angry man stared from her to him and muttered, "Pretty cocky now, aren't you? You've got the dog, and you've got the girl. You must think life is pretty damn sweet." All of a sudden, he had a gun in his hand. "Well, guess what?" he began, waving the gun. "Life ain't that sweet. In fact, life is a bitch, and, if you don't figure it out when you're young, the world eats you up and spits you out."

Baron asked, "Did you wake up on the wrong side of the bed today?"

Brittany muttered, "More like he's always on the wrong side of it."

"Shut the fuck up, and don't you fucking dare ask any questions. Don't you get in my face about anything," he raged. "I'm here for a reason, and I'm not leaving until I find it."

She considered him for a moment, then told Baron, "He does sound a little on the sincere side."

"Yeah, ya think?" the angry gunman snapped. "You told me that you were here for your lost dog, and now you've got your dog, so get the hell out, and take your injured, weak-ass boyfriend with you."

At that, Baron stiffened, but then relaxed. In a lazy tone, he replied, "I see you're one of *those guys*. One of the punks who sits on the sidelines and knocks everybody else for doing their duty?"

"Oh God, save me, will you?" he yelled, with a mocking look. "Get lost or this bullet will find another sorry ass to land in."

"Another one?" Brittany asked. "Have you already shot someone today?"

He glared at her.

"Yeah, he probably shot his partner," Baron muttered ever-so-softly—but not as softly as he thought.

The other man spun fast. "What was that about a partner?"

"We ran into a man here last night, looking for his partner," Baron explained. "Not too gentle either, so it seems like maybe you're a perfect match."

"Where was he?" he asked.

She pointed to where they'd found the downed officers last night. "He was over there." She then waved her hands. "Wait, why? Are you missing a partner?"

He just glared at her, his gaze searching. "Get lost. I've got work to do." And, with that, he took several steps backward, motioned with the gun, and said, "Go." Then he turned and hurried away, as if he needed to get out of here and fast.

She watched as Kingston and Baron took several steps in the direction the man had gone. She reached out and grabbed his hand. "No, no, no, no."

He frowned at her. "You do realize that these two gunmen seem to be from out of town and are looking for something. They both are probably intent on stealing whatever it is that they came here for."

"I no longer care," she replied. "Whatever is between these two gunmen, that's their problem. And, if it involves whatever was here even before the hurricane started this nightmare, that's also not our problem."

He flashed a bright smile at her. "What? So, you want to go back home, where it's safe and sound, and not try to solve this mystery?"

She nodded emphatically. "Yes, that is absolutely what I want to do, but, for that, we have to be alive."

CHAPTER 11

BRITTANY HAD NOT been kidding. Absolutely nothing was good about this scenario, and this latest gunman was more than a nightmare, and she didn't want to deal with him ever again. She looked back at Baron, as they walked toward his truck. "Besides," she added, "we have another patient in need of attention."

He frowned at her but followed along, as she led the way back over to where Kingston had taken her earlier—to the mama dog and her puppies. Her heart melted a little more, as Baron bent down and cooed at the mama dog. She let him pick up her puppies and examine them, her tail wagging the entire time.

"Well, she wasn't anywhere near as welcoming to me," she noted in fascination.

He looked over at her and smiled. "I have a way with dogs."

"Yes, I can see that," she stated. "I'll just reiterate that I think you should put that gift to good use."

"Heard you the first twelve times," he teased, with laughter in his tone.

She nodded. "Yet you're still ignoring me."

"Nope, I'll take it all into consideration," he clarified, with a smile as he looked over at her. "But, right now, this lady and her babies need to get checked over, and then we need to find a place for all of them to go." He looked at her and asked, "Do you have room for them?"

"For how long?" she asked cautiously, as she stared down at the pups.

"The puppies need eight weeks at least, but twelve would be better for mama's sake and for all of their well-being really."

"I have a big yard and an empty basement."

"Done," he declared. "Besides, you'll find very quickly that they'll break your heart."

"Yes, that's part of the problem," she admitted, as she stared at him. "I'm really not into broken hearts."

He grinned and shook his head. "This is a different kind of broken heart, but trust me that you'll be fine."

"If you say so," she muttered, with a sigh.

The two of them picked up the box of puppies, but the mama dog didn't get up. Brittany watched Baron's facial expression, when the mama dog just lay there. "That can't be good, can it?"

"No, it means she's most likely hurt," he suggested.

Brittany cast her glance back to where the angry stranger had been. "What about him?"

"I already texted Badger, and he's contacted local law enforcement. I'm sure they'll be tardy as usual, but, if nothing else, they can't have somebody out here, waving a gun around."

"Sure," she agreed, "but we also have the issue of whoever owns this place."

"True," he replied, shaking his head, "but that's an issue for another day. As for now, you're right. We need to get this little lady some attention."

It took a bit to get her loaded into the vehicle, all the

puppies intact, and to get Kingston up in there too. The War Dog didn't want to sit in the front of the truck but with the mama dog in the back.

"Kingston's really protective of her, isn't he?" she wondered.

"He is, and that's not a bad thing." They made it to the vet hospital. Baron made two trips, very carefully carrying the boxful of puppies inside, then went back for the mama dog.

The vet took one look, raced over, and grabbed a gurney. "What happened to her?"

"Not sure, but we came from the closed-off area at the beach, where the hurricane struck, and we found her and her babies among the debris."

The vet nodded. "Ah, poor baby. Whether the birth was brought on because of the disaster or was delayed until she got free and could give birth, I don't know," he shared. "Give me a little bit to sort her out."

Brittany and Baron sat in the lobby and waited. She kept getting up and pacing and then sitting back down again.

Baron looked over at her, as she plunked down beside him. "She'll be fine, you know."

"How can you be sure?"

"I can't be certain," he conceded, "but I'm willing to go on faith that she'll be fine."

She smiled. "That's just because you're a nice man."

"That's what you said about my brother."

"Your brother was a very nice man."

"Oh, oh, I see how it is," he said in a joking manner. "Brad was a *very nice* man. Me? I'm just a run-of-the-mill nice man."

She groaned. "You're just trying to distract me."

"Is it working?"

"No," she snapped, and then sighed. "Yes, it is."

He laughed. "Good, at least that's one thing I'm doing right."

"You're doing everything right."

"Yet it's so messed up that I got my head cracked, and I don't even know why."

She frowned at that. "We should have gone to the hospital to have them look you over."

"It's okay," Baron said yet again. "I'm feeling a lot better, and the headache's gone."

She looked over at him and raised one eyebrow. "You're lying." The grin that flashed across his face confirmed that she'd caught him in that lie too. "What is it about guys not wanting to get themselves checked out?"

"I don't know," he replied, with a shrug. "Maybe it has to do with needles and doctors and all that stuff," he quipped, with a mock grin.

"I highly doubt you give a crap about any of that."

"Oh, you would be surprised," he noted, with a smile. "I've watched some of the biggest and the toughest badass men become an absolute jelly blob over a needle pinch."

"Really?" she asked.

He nodded. "Hey, phobias are phobias, and it can even happen to the biggest men you can imagine," he explained. "All kinds are in the military. It was interesting to see. Yet it was sad because, if anybody found out, they would be teased mercilessly."

"What about you?"

"Oh, I don't care about needles so much," he shared. "It's a *whatever* for me. I must have it, so I have it, but not everybody can enjoy that same freedom," he murmured.

"For some people it really was a problem."

An odd silence fell over them. She stared over at him for a moment and then it clicked. "Oh my God, you're thinking about going back over there, aren't you?"

That same damn crooked smile flashed, and he shrugged. "It's not so much that I'm thinking about it, as much as I never stopped thinking about it."

She frowned. "But you have no real reason to go back, do you?"

He looked over at her. "You've got a box of your grandmother's things there, don't you?"

She nodded. "But I can get those another day, and, if we don't get them, we don't get them," she declared, raising both hands. "My grandma was pretty adamant about not putting myself into further danger over it." He nodded, and yet it didn't seem to satisfy him. "And if you're looking for permission or for an excuse," she added in a droll tone, "I don't think you need me to provide it."

"No, I don't," he agreed. "I'm just unsettled over a lot of the scenarios I have seen here."

"So, why do I feel like there's more to it? Is there?"

He studied her, then shrugged. "Maybe, maybe not. I'm not exactly sure what is going on here at the moment."

She settled back and waited. When the vet returned and informed them that the mama dog and her puppies could all be taken home, Brittany turned to Baron, with a questioning gaze. "So, my place?"

He nodded. "If you're okay with that."

"Well, I'm the only one who has a livable place. I've seen your brother's place. It took some damage, but it looks like it could be easily repaired."

"It did look like it could be repaired." He nodded.

"Yeah, I do need to take another look at that though, to see what changes must be made."

"And talk to the insurance company," she pointed out.

"I've definitely got to talk to the insurance people. Something I probably should have done already. Although I think my mother would have already started in on that."

"Will she move into Brad's house?"

"No, she has her own house and never wanted to be that close to the beach."

"So, the house could potentially be yours."

"It is mine. Brad has always been very clear about that. The house didn't seem to have been hit too badly, but, if the insurance company doesn't want me in there, well, you know how that goes."

"Right, well, you'll have to make that decision too," she noted.

He didn't say much more. As they loaded up the pups, she asked him, "How do we find out who she belongs to?"

"Or if she belongs to anybody," he corrected her. "My brother was also fostering a bunch of dogs, and, for all I know, she was part of that."

"Oh, wow, I never considered that," she replied. "What if she doesn't have a family?" She looked at their group of animals and realized that, once again, her comfort zone had been pushed out a little bit further than she was comfortable with.

He chuckled. "I'm sure we can find homes for them, but we have plenty of time to consider that. Let's get them settled in. She needs to know that she and her puppies are safe."

At that, Brittany's heart melted because the most important thing for the dog right now was to know she had a safe place to raise her puppies. "Well, my place it is then."

And, with that, they headed to her house. As Kingston, Baron, and Brittany all wandered around the backyard, checking to ensure it was secure enough for the dogs to be in, Baron nodded. "This is pretty good."

"It's pretty good, but it's not great," she muttered. "I mean, it's all right. It's just not as pretty or as nice as it could be."

He glanced over at her, a wry look on his face. "This is so much better than the places she has been."

Brittany winced at that thought.

"The biggest thing is making sure she's safe here, and now she is. We'll just need to rig up a spot for her to be out of the weather."

She shook her head. "I have the basement and also that big porch that's partially closed off."

He walked through to the door she mentioned, then stepped outside and took a look. Turning back, he looked at her and nodded. "This is perfect."

"You think it'll work?" she asked anxiously. "I really don't have much experience with animals and what they need."

"I think this will be wonderful for her," he stated warmly, "at least on a temporary basis, while the pups are small. It will do just fine."

"That's good to know," she muttered. "I am really not sure how much of this long-term stuff I can consider."

He chuckled. "Don't worry about it, at least not right now."

"Yeah, you say that, but then you disappear, and I'm left with six puppies and a mama dog that needs to be fixed."

"That she does." Baron frowned, turning to look back at

the mama dog.

As if realizing she was the subject of curiosity, the mama dog got up slowly from where they had placed her in the backyard and walked around, sniffing appreciatively. Kingston was beside her all the way.

"Look. She seems better already," Baron pointed out. "Nothing quite like seeing an animal back up on its feet to realize that's the more normal state."

The mama dog found a corner and went to the bathroom, then slowly walked back and nuzzled her puppies. Then Kingston came over and nuzzled her. The two of them greeted each other like long-lost friends, which made Brittany stop and take note. "You think they knew each other?"

"Well, if they didn't, they do now," he stated. "Animals deal with things very quickly, whether being very accepting or rejecting unwanted attention. In the wild or in the packs on the streets, sick or injured animals are often left behind because they slow down the pack. It's cruel, and it's seemingly a horrific way to go, but it's to save the rest of the animals."

"Which is a horrible thing," she declared.

"I know, but it doesn't change the fact that Mother Nature has reasons for everything she does, and the bottom line is continuity of the species."

She winced at that, while the mama dog settled back into the box and closed her eyes, as the puppies nursed. "She's not very strong, is she?"

"No, she isn't," Baron noted. "I suspect she was abused and is suffering. She could have been a popular dog, for all we know, but the hurricane really did a number on her. Whatever happened, we don't have any history on her. I have yet to check my brother's house to see if he has any records that might help sort through some of what was going on in his world," Baron mentioned, "but I'll try to get in there today and do that. Are you okay to stay here with her? Even if I take Kingston with me?"

Brittany stared at him for a long moment. "Did you decide that I should stay here to look after her just to keep me out of trouble?"

"I'm hoping you'll stay here because I'm still a little worried that she's not out of the woods. She had a normal delivery it seems, but she's still under a lot of stress, and it's obvious she's not had an easy time of it. Therefore, if you were to stay with her, I think it would help her. Yet, if you're not up for it, just tell me."

"Then what? Will you stay with her?" she asked.

"It means I'll make my trip a whole lot shorter. I'll try to find what I'm looking for at Brad's house, maybe make some quick damage assessments, and then be back here in an hour."

"An hour won't allow you very much time to do that," she muttered. "Why don't you make it three or four hours … or longer if need be."

"That's a compromise I can live with. Deal." He walked over, stroked the mama dog's head. "While I'm gone, come up with a name for her." And, with that, he let Kingston in the front seat, then he hopped in the truck and took off.

He left her staring at the mama dog, who even now was looking at Brittany beseechingly—as if asking, begging her for a home.

"Oh no, you don't," she muttered. "I have no experience with dogs. I don't know the first thing about them."

It had always been this way. Her mother had claimed to

be highly allergic to dogs and cats. Thus Brittany's childhood had been denied a furry pet. Then it just became commonplace for her to continue to live without a four-legged companion—even now, living in her own house, with her mother long gone, even with Grandma and Pocket living close by Brittany.

Looking back now, Brittany wondered whether her mother had been honest or just not wanted another responsibility dumped into her lap. Yet animals had always liked Brittany, and they always came to her for a cuddle or a visit or to garner some treat. Brittany now suspected that she would have to learn very quickly how to handle the full-time care of this mama dog and her six puppies.

BARON KNEW BRITTANY'S reticence over the animals had literally been just a lack of experience, and he could understand that. Also perhaps an element of fear could be detected in Brittany, while she still doubted herself, both about her former unhealthy eating habits and more recently about her selection of a potential husband.

Baron could see how Brittany might not consider herself the best person to look after another living being, especially when she still felt that she had failed herself on two key issues. Not an easy thing for anyone to deal with, even one problem at a time, but now add to that the worry about looking after her grandmother? Yeah, Brittany could be really questioning herself.

She didn't see the good things even now, and that was something Baron wanted to help her with. He wanted something more for her. She was incredibly strong and resilient and had been through a lot of trauma and was doing incredibly well. He wanted her to see what he saw and all the good things that she had done for herself. He wanted her to be confident in her own right, and to let go of worrying about what everybody else might still be considering, expecting Brittany to fail again. This was a classic example of the pros and cons of a small town.

As he drove, his mother called, and he tapped the Speakerphone button on his cell. As he turned onto the beaten-up road, he saw more neighbors heading down into the subdivision again, as if looking for more of their things.

"Where are you?" his mother asked, her tone anxious.

"I'm heading down to Brad's house. Why? Are you okay?" he asked sharply.

"Oh, … it's okay," she muttered. "Nothing to be so alarmed about. It's just been a rough couple days."

"It's been a rough couple weeks," he pointed out.

"You're right. … It's so hard to believe he's gone."

"I know."

"And what about you? Will you pack up and leave again?"

"I'm not sure what I'm doing. Technically the house is mine, and I assume it can be repaired."

"Have you been to the place?"

"That's one of the things I'll go take a look at today," he shared. "I can't promise that it'll be livable. And I can't promise that I'm staying, but it is something I'm considering."

"Really?" she asked, hope in her tone.

He nodded, but she of course couldn't see it. "Yes, but no guarantees though."

"No, of course not," she muttered. "I just feel like this

damn town is taking everything from me."

"Is there any other place you want to live? Because, if so, this would be a good time to make that move."

"I don't have any place else to go and no friends to go with," she said. "Your brother was all I had."

Baron winced once again at the reminder that he hadn't been the son his mother got along with, and that she'd lost the one son she had really cared about. "I'm sorry for that," he replied, striving for neutrality, though inside it was still a blow. Even as a thirty-six-year-old man, that shit hurt. He shook his head to shake it off. "I'll take a good look at the house today and see what issues I'll have."

"I did phone the insurance company, and they should be coming out to assess the damage as soon as they are allowed into the area."

"That would be good," he murmured, "because I definitely saw some damage to assess. Listen. I'll talk to you later, Ma. Be safe." With that he hung up and tried to drag his thoughts and emotions back under control. He headed straight to his brother's house.

As he drove, he realized Brad's house was just one, possibly two houses over from the creepy house that everybody had been talking about. The very one that had been attracting the attention of the two strange gunmen.

Baron pondered all that, as he got out of his vehicle, let Kingston out from the back, and walked toward the entrance. The front door still stood, and the roof was still on, which was a good start. Yet he definitely saw some damage, and who knew what part of Brad's house may collapse in the interim. Still, the hurricane damage to Brad's house wasn't nearly as extensive as some of the other houses on the same block. Some had been reduced to random piles of wreckage, too far gone to be salvaged, whereas his brother's home seemed hardly touched in comparison.

Baron smiled as he considered that, thinking maybe he could stay here after all. Pulling out his phone, he started making notes of things that might need to be fixed. He would get some professionals out to see how stable and secure various parts of the structure were, so he could be prepared for conversations with the insurance company.

As he walked farther inside, he realized that, all in all, a lot could be said for the old days, when things were built and meant to last, because this house had come through the hurricane better than most.

Baron smiled as he saw a bunch of his brother's old mementoes and realized that staying here would entail a memory clean out at the same time. Yet it also might be fun reacquainting himself with his brother. It would be a tough thing to do regardless and would need to get done to some degree, whether he stayed here or sold the house, but he was up for the job.

As he wandered through the downstairs, he headed into the back, where Brad's office was located. It was a mess. He stopped in the doorway and winced. One of the windows was broken, and papers were strewn across the floor.

He stepped up to the desk, sat in the weather-beaten old chair, pulled it up against the desk, and opened a couple drawers. Most of them were empty, and then he noted a pattern to the mess.

Drawers had been emptied and tossed on the floor. Not only had every drawer been emptied but several of the drawers were still upside down on top of the paperwork on the floor. Slowly standing, Baron assessed it with fresh eyes, adding to the growing fear he'd been sensing but hadn't been able to prove.

Fear that something had gone wrong in his brother's world.

Baron slowly walked over to the broken window, noting that the hurricane had provided a hell of an excuse for the place to appear to be ransacked. Yet, as he studied the damage to the window clasp, he realized this was most likely a classic breaking-and-entering scenario. The hurricane would have blown out the glass and windowsill, not the locks. It would certainly not have left the glass intact.

Also his brother's house had been generally spared a good share of the hurricane damage, which made it interesting to see that just the window in the office area had been affected.

Baron sat back down again and sighed. "Brad, what were you up to? What did you know or have that somebody else wanted? Or what was going on in your world that you may or may not have even known about and that somebody else was afraid you did?"

Baron's mind kept grasping for all kinds of theoretical answers. Yet the only thing that came back as being logical was the idea that the B&E was somehow connected to the two gunmen who had been driving them crazy lately. However, even that didn't sound normal to him.

He sifted through the paperwork on the floor, seeing if anything caught his eye. His brother did a ton of volunteer work, yet Baron didn't see very much of that reflected in this paperwork. Other than that, Baron found receipts for dog food, utility bills, and even some for mileage he had apparently been keeping track of. It just looked like typical small-business receipts.

He slowly sorted through what he found, knowing that

he would have to file income tax for his brother as well. As he continued to sort through the remaining paperwork, another pattern emerged.

This was all about Brad's search and rescue business and the things that were important in his life. So, for Brad, that was the animals. Baron smiled at that because that was so totally Brad.

The animals would come first, which also meant that, if Brad had no money, the animals would get fed first. Baron had known many people like that. Thankfully his brother should never have been in a stage in life where he needed to make a choice between one or the other. Brad should have been fine and should have been able to feed all of them with no problem. If not, he damn well should have reached out, and Baron would have helped him.

As he continued to shuffle through the documents, he found a couple bank statements, reflecting a modest sum in the bank account. Enough to fix a few things around the house that needed attention. Baron had been subsidizing his mother's low income for quite a while. He'd been a late baby for her and not necessarily a welcome one at that. Thus his belated birth had been a hard road for her, particularly after his father had passed. Plus it had also been part of the reason she had been so much closer to Brad.

It had been just the two of them for a very long time, until Baron had made his unplanned arrival. Not that it was his fault by any means, but Ma hadn't had an easy time after his birth.

As he worked his way through the paperwork, sorting it out as he went, he could see that his brother hadn't had an easy time of it either, but had always made ends meet, which was very much his brother. Baron straightened out what he could, and, when he came across a set of photos, he stopped and smiled.

There were snapshots of the house, photos of his mother laughing while visiting Brad, which included all the animals running around the backyard. That reminded Baron that he had to check the fencing, ensure it was still secure before he brought any animals here. That way he could certainly take on the ones currently at Brittany's house.

She would probably thoroughly enjoy the opportunity to look after them, once she got used to it, but she was still hesitant, and he could understand that. He had spent a lifetime with animals, mostly because his father was forever bringing home strays, much to his mother's disgust, he was sure. That had more or less stopped once his father had passed, but Ma's two boys had been out there trying to help almost every animal imaginable.

His father had been a good person, and his brother was cut from the same cloth. It must have been horrific for his mother to endure the losses she had sustained, especially now with both of them gone. She was also that much older now. Not hugely so, not quite Brittany's grandmother's age, but Ma was in her early seventies.

As far as Baron knew, Ma was in good health, but he probably wouldn't have been told if she wasn't, which was a timely thought as he came across his brother's medical records in a file sitting off to the side. He picked it up, took a look, and winced.

His brother had been in a rapidly worsening failing heart situation for a while, knowing perfectly well that he could do nothing about it.

"Why the hell didn't you say something?" Baron muttered to the empty room. "I would have been here as much as I could have."

But it had always seemed as if there was more time. He wondered if everybody who lost someone had the same regrets at the end of the day. Always thinking they had time to fix things, time to make up for lost time, another day to make things all work out. That had certainly been his experience, but maybe other people didn't have all these regrets. Maybe it was just him. Baron winced at that thought.

Once he glanced through the rest of the paperwork, he found another folder, and this one had his mother's name on it. Slowly he picked it up and opened it, then started swearing. She hadn't told him anything about having cancer or the treatments that his brother had taken her to on a regular basis.

No wonder she was so devastated at losing Brad. Now she would have to talk to Baron about it, and that wasn't something she would ever want to do. She was very proud and hated spilling dirty laundry. Yet something like this shouldn't be thought of in that way. His mother needed help, and she hadn't told him. It was one more blow in a long line of blows that Baron had thought he had dealt with. Staring at the file in front of him, he realized he hadn't dealt with life as he should have.

"Well, damn it, Brad. You really could have told me, even if she wouldn't," he muttered.

He went through the file carefully, taking the time required to understand what was going on and to realize that he would have a conversation with her fairly quickly. She had undergone multiple treatments, had come through them, but now the most recent report that his brother had at the top of the stack documented the cancer's reoccurrence.

The report basically told Baron that he would lose his mother, after having just lost his brother. Baron sat here for a long moment, shaken by this unexpected turn of news.

"Well, damn it," he muttered. "Would anybody ever tell me? Or was everybody just waiting until it happened and then would say, *Oh yeah, sorry, dude. She knew about it but didn't want you to know?*"

Well, now she didn't have a choice because he knew.

Getting up slowly and feeling the oldest he had ever felt, he headed into the kitchen and discovered that one of the windows had blown open, causing some wind and rain damage inside the home, but nothing that couldn't be cleaned up. He quickly straightened things up. As he stared around, he had absolutely no reason why he couldn't stay here himself from now on.

Baron knew that Brad had always hoped he'd move in and to stay here for the last few years of his life. That had always been part of the plan. Baron hadn't exactly made too many long-term plans for himself, particularly not after his injury. His brother had been there for him, but Baron's recovery wasn't anything he wanted his brother to hang around and to lose time on. It seemed they were all stubbornly and fiercely independent.

He had told Brad repeatedly that, as soon as Baron was back on his feet, he would come down for a visit. Brad had been pretty blunt about Baron's attitude, telling him to forget about getting back on his feet before he came home, that plenty of people were around to help him.

Baron questioned that now, since it didn't appear that they had been there to help his brother. Swearing at the lost opportunities and wishing for a chance at a redo, Baron put on a pot of coffee, smiling at the thought that he had electricity and could even do such a simple everyday thing, after expecting the house to be halfway destroyed. So far the damages downstairs were all minor, and the insurance shouldn't have a problem handling it.

Minutes later, with a cup of hot coffee in hand, he wandered upstairs to the bedrooms, Kingston sticking close to his side, estimating what work would be needed up here. Once upstairs, he took a look around and frowned. It had been tossed, as in literally tossed by man, not by the hurricane. He set his brother's bedroom to rights, as Baron questioned what anyone could have possibly cared about in this room. In the night table drawers, still on the floor, were a bunch of dog photos tossed randomly into the drawer. It was as if the burglar had taken out the packet of snapshots, checked through each one, then just dumped them back into the drawer.

Anybody who expected his brother to have anything other than dog photos didn't know him as well as they should have. But what was the intruder looking for?

What could anybody possibly be looking for in Brad's house?

As he turned, he stepped up to the window. He saw houses in the distance, and that included the spooky Gorman house. Now that was a consideration. Did somebody worry about Brad seeing something? Had Brad been seen taking photos of something in the neighborhood? What could possibly have interested anybody about Brad's life?

No answers were evident in this room, but Baron got the suspicion, stronger than ever, that all was not as it seemed. Whether it was something Brad had even realized was an issue, Baron didn't know. Up until now, Kingston had been at his side, happy to wander and nuzzle up against him, only to lie down until Baron was ready to move on to the next room. But suddenly the dog stood and ran downstairs, barking.

"What do you want, buddy?" Baron went to find him at the back door, still barking. "Need to go out for a few minutes?" When he opened the door and stepped outside, the dog bolted forward. Instead of heading out to the backyard to do his business, he bolted around the corner of the house and started barking again. Baron raced around the house just in time to see the dog jumping up at the fence, but it was just a shade too high. In Kingston's prime War Dog days, he would have managed that jump of the tall fence without a problem. However, now with the many broken legs the dog had sustained, plus the pins now put in multiple places, it was a challenge.

Baron moved over to the fence and hauled himself up. He watched a man running away in the distance. Baron didn't know for sure that this particular man had been in his backyard, but, given Kingston's reaction, it was quite likely. "Well, buddy, what did we get into, *huh?*"

Kingston barked at him.

"I know, but we're not exactly prepared to run down there after him."

On the other hand, if this guy had any idea that Baron had been here at the house—though how could he not, since the truck was parked out front? Maybe the stranger had been surprised to find them here and inside the home. "What was he thinking?" Had the man been the one who had tossed the place but now came back for another look? Was he expecting Baron himself to have found whatever it was the stranger had been looking for?

Baron had no clue what anybody was after from Brad's

house or why anybody even would care. This just puzzled him even further.

His phone rang just then, and he looked down to see it was Brittany. "Hey. Well, the good news is that my brother's house is in very decent shape."

"Oh gosh, that's wonderful," she cried out.

"It's livable right now."

"You think so? I just heard that they were finishing up the safety checks and that we should be allowed back in pretty soon."

"That's good news, … certainly for me. I think maybe I'll just move in here."

"Really?" she asked. "I mean, is it really that untouched?"

"It's in so much better shape than other homes nearby, which is amazing. When I was here before, I only saw the outside damage, but, after taking a closer look, the damage inside? … Well, it appears to be largely manmade."

"Oh, those damn looters," she grumbled. "I hope they didn't take everything."

"I'm not sure what they were looking for, but they didn't take anything that I can see. Not the usual stuff anyway. The TV is still here, as are several appliances, so I don't know what they would have been after," he noted. "Yet the desk in the home office has been tossed, with all the drawers pulled out, and the same thing was done in the master bedroom. The night tables, every drawer in there had been stripped. Just from the way I found it, somebody came here, looking for something specific, and was systematically going through everything to ensure they found it."

"Do you think they did find it though?" she asked curiously. "I can't imagine what Brad would have been hiding."

"I'm not sure he was hiding anything, as such, but maybe he just picked up something nobody else wanted him to. He spent hours and hours wandering these areas, whether searching for lost people or dogs, or cleaning up the beachfront, or planting trees or whatever."

"Yes," she agreed. "I remember all that. He used to come around with garbage bags and collect all the trash that the young kids used to leave on the roadsides or at the beach. He used to tell them off every time they would leave behind their trash, and they would laugh and just drop more in front of him."

"*Great,* so he was not as well-loved as you would have me believe."

"He was, absolutely he was, at least by the older folks. He was just considered a little *off* as far as the rest of the community was concerned. The townsfolk didn't understand how he made money, since he didn't really work, not the standard nine-to-five job. Yet he did a ton of rescue work. … So people just didn't quite understand him. But they did care about him, and he was well loved. Don't you dare think anything different."

"Right," he said, as he walked back into the house. "Kingston just caused quite a ruckus, and somebody may have been in the backyard."

"Seriously?" She gasped.

"I don't know for certain. That's the problem. I don't really understand what someone could have been looking for. Thus it's hard for me to know if they were just here or if the person I saw running away had nothing to do with it."

"And yet …" she added in a dour tone.

"And yet it feels very much like they were specifically here, either checking out the house or checking out my presence to see what I was up to."

"Well, you be careful," she said in alarm. "Are you coming back here anytime soon?"

"I was just checking on the fence, and I think the dogs can probably come here," he suggested. "It appears to be safe enough for that."

"It's not safe enough until we know for sure you're safe," she pointed out. "Not if you've got people running through your house."

"It could just be looters, and, once everybody starts moving back in again, that should ease up somewhat."

"Maybe," she agreed, "but what about those two gunmen who were down there? They were scary."

He chuckled. "They were scary, and I won't lie. They were definitely serious and up to no good, but that doesn't mean they'll come back."

"I don't know about that," she murmured. "It seems very likely that they'll be back."

"Do you have any reason for saying that?" he asked lightly, yet knowing full well that his instincts had saved his ass more than a few times.

"I don't know. … It just seems to be unfinished business to me."

He agreed but didn't want to say that to her. "Let me finish checking over the fence line and see what else I can see around here. I did make some coffee," he shared, "and something was so reassuring about being able to make coffee in your own space."

"So, will you stay now?" she asked in a teasing tone. "I mean, it's not a bad deal, getting the house to yourself, especially if it's not been trashed by the hurricane."

"Yeah, but I would leave it in a minute to have my

brother back here instead," he pointed out.

"I didn't mean it that way. I'm sorry."

"I know. I know you didn't, and having my brother's house will be great, but it definitely needs some work, but not just from recent events."

"I wondered about that, since he never seemed to put any time into fixing up the house."

"I didn't ever talk to him about it, but he always seemed to be pretty happy with it just the way it was. The hurricane damage and the intruder mess may be minimal, but the house needed maintenance work long before that."

"I get that. … I thought the same about my grandma and her place."

"I also found Brad's medical records, and he wasn't doing very well, worse than I was led to believe. So I'm pretty sure he didn't consider making any of the changes or upgrades to the house a priority, since he always intended this house to be mine when he was gone. I almost expect to find a letter from him that would explain *something*. … I don't know why."

"Well, keep looking," she murmured, "because, if you find a letter, it will be worth everything, particularly when you never got a chance to say goodbye. Let me know when you leave there, and I'll put on something to eat for us here."

"Sounds good," he replied.

In the distance, he heard Kingston again. Stepping out to the backyard, he was once again barking at the fence line and glaring at Baron for not understanding. "Come on, buddy." He walked over to the fence again, hopped up a little bit so he could look over but saw nothing.

"I'm sorry, Kingston. We won't go on a chase right now. Let's go back inside." The thought of a letter or something from his brother made a whole lot of sense. If such a thing existed, Baron really wanted to find it.

He headed back to the office, but he had already gone through most of the materials while he was in here earlier. The only other place he hadn't been to yet was the spare bedroom, which was technically Baron's, since that's where he stayed whenever he came here to visit. He'd been on so many missions, nearly back-to-back, that he had used this as his home base when he wasn't otherwise deployed, which also gave him a place to come and visit his family. He was still struggling with the information about his mother's health and the knowledge that he would lose the last of his family soon.

As he wandered into his bedroom, he looked up to see the same stars that his brother had put up in his bedroom so long ago. This had been their childhood home, and that was something else Baron had never quite understood either. How did Brad end up with it? Maybe Ma didn't want to stay here because his father had passed away in this house. Baron remembered vague details and his brother telling him that the house would be Baron's, whenever it was time.

As he stared around his childhood room, his gaze landed on some paperwork that had fallen to the floor. He picked it up, and his heart lurched as he read the cover letter.

Dear Baron, if you're reading this, it's time for me to say goodbye. Yet, in truth, I should have said goodbye a very long time ago. I was trying to get Mom through her cancer treatments, and don't be mad, but she didn't want you to know. It was more that she didn't want you to worry, and she didn't want you to come home to look after her.

I don't know where we're at in terms of that stage

of her life. I can only hope that she is still okay and can enjoy a few more years. If not, … I'm sorry, bro, because that means both of us are gone.

Baron stopped and took a deep breath, as his brother's letter continued.

Everything here is fine and dandy. The house needs work, and, as you'll see, I've only done the bare minimum. Sorry, bro. Looking after the house was not on the plan because that was never my thing. Since it wasn't Dad's either, the house definitely could use some work. I'm not exactly leaving you a whole lot in terms of an inheritance either. You get the family home, and it's been a good one for me. I hope it'll also be a good one for you.

I know that you're not coming home in the same shape that you left, but you've never been one to run away from responsibilities. At least this is a place that you know and can call yours, if we survive climate change or all the other doomsday forecasting that's going on.

Just enough of his brother's humor filled these words that it made Baron smile. He sagged down onto the bed and kept reading.

I've been helping one of the old neighbors here. He's getting on and not doing so well, but he's also having some issues. Now that the old guy had to go in for some surgery, I promised I would look after things for him, including taking care of Kingston, the War Dog. Then fate stepped in, and I needed to be in the hospital, so the old guy got the War Dog back. Then we knew that the hurricane was on its way, and that is one of the reasons I'm writing this letter. My last checkup wasn't good, and the doctor gave me weeks, not months, and that was already weeks ago. So I don't know at what point in time I just won't wake up one day.

But please consider looking after the animals. I've got a couple dogs that come and go, though I don't know what will be here when you are reading this. I've got a pregnant female that was abused, and I've been working with her, trying to get her to the point where we can reestablish a home for her somewhere else, but, if not, well, she stays with me forever. She's just that kind of a dog. Kingston is also pretty attached to her, and, since I've had him here, the two of them have become quite close.

There was a wrinkled spot on the letter, and Baron wondered if his brother had shed a tear while writing this part. Just the thought broke his own heart.

I'm sorry, bro. I had always hoped we would have some time together before this event came, but no point in telling you, since you were dealing with your own injuries and trying to get back on your feet. I know you're coming, and maybe this will all blow over, and I can tell you in person, but I can't promise that.

As it is, the old guy across the way, who looks after Kingston, told me a strange story. I'm not sure I believe him, but he seems to think that, if he doesn't come out of this alive, some restitution needed to happen. So, I put this letter in our hidey-hole. It's pretty damn strange that I did this, but I figured it might be up your alley to try and fix. I'm waiting for you to come back before I even consider tackling it myself. And, if I'm not here to tackle it with you, well, it will all be on you. I'm sorry again, but please remember that I love you and that you were never, ever unwanted. I know that's always been a thing for you, but you were and still are loved. If I'm not here to greet you as you come home, just know that I'll be watching over you from above.

Your loving brother.

Baron sat here for what seemed like hours, but then he heard Kingston barking like crazy again, this time in the front yard. He folded the letter and put it in his pocket, as he raced downstairs. Kingston was circling the truck like a madman and kept bumping the side of the truck.

Baron quickly closed the front door and ran to him. Then Kingston ran off, still barking, at a speed that raised the hairs on his arms. Definitely something was wrong. Seriously wrong.

CHAPTER 12

B RITTANY WANDERED AROUND her place aimlessly, finding herself stopping beside the mama dog's new bed constantly. Brittany had pulled blankets out of storage and ended up creating way more than the poor dog needed, but something was absolutely lovely about having her here. Brittany had been so reticent at first, and she didn't know why. Maybe it was because she now knew that she would likely lose the mama dog and her puppies.

She followed the mama dog outside and sat down beside the dog and rubbed her ears. Seeing her flinch made Brittany fear the dog had likely been abused, yet here she was, still valiant and strong.

"Something can be said about those of us who come through the worst that life has to offer," she whispered to the dog, as she stroked her. "Your life has taken a really good turn now, so you'll be fine."

She wouldn't be at all surprised if Brad had picked this one up from somewhere and had already been working with her. The fact that nobody else knew about all that Brad did for these animals also didn't mean it wasn't one of the dogs that he had living with him. Brittany didn't know what dogs he had at any given time, but he was always working to help someone, even though his own situation was beyond help.

She wondered about going through life knowing you

could die any day, only to stop and laugh because that was the truth for everyone. The reality was that any person could go at any time. They could simply just not wake up one morning, yet everybody expected to live long and healthy lives. However, in Brad's case, he never had that opportunity, and that must have been devastating for him. Somehow he had come to a certain level of peace and had found a way to live with it. She had to admire that about him too.

Everybody had known he had major health issues, but whenever he did something they thought was rude or strange—which for the kids was as simple as picking up garbage on the beach—they all said Brad had a mental health issue. She'd never seen anything like that about him, so hadn't considered such a thing.

She also thought that Baron would not take kindly to people making those kinds of conjectures about Brad either. Yet Baron would empathize when people did it though, because he appeared to be very much on the understanding side. But she also knew he was struggling with the loss of Brad, plus Baron appeared to be under some strain or stress involving his mother. Brittany remembered the rumors that Baron had been a very late baby for her.

She couldn't imagine going through a pregnancy well into her late forties. That would have been rough on Baron's mother, and his father as well, although Brittany remembered him as being a big, jovial man, full of laughter and life. He seemed a complete opposite to his wife, who had more of a dour personality and rarely smiled. However, the few times Brittany had seen her out with Brad, the two of them always appeared to be comfortable and happy together, and, for that, Brittany was grateful.

Everybody should have somebody in their world, and

Brad appeared to be that for his mother, and her for him. Brittany didn't want to think about what that meant in terms of Baron's feelings, but Brittany could only worry about so many people at any given time. She reached down and stroked Lucky's face. This mama dog had been lucky to have survived, so it was a good name for her. Lucky stretched out willingly and turned up her belly. Brittany spent a few minutes just rubbing her soft fur and smiling at her.

"You'll be fine," she kept reassuring her. "You and your puppies will be just fine." She sighed, enjoying the dogs and the nice weather outside today.

When a man broke through her happy reverie, she was shocked as hell.

"Shit, get over the dog already, will you?"

She stiffened to stare at the stranger who had just hopped over the fence in front of her. She looked at her fence and then back at him. "A fence is there for a reason."

"Yeah, I know." He sauntered toward her, and, as he got closer, she realized who it was. The angry man threatening to kill Kingston. The angry armed man who had followed her when she ran. The color fled from her face as she stared at him in shock. "What the hell do you want?"

"Ah, so you do remember me, don't you? A part of me says yay, and another part of me says something else, but the bottom line is that it sucks to be you," he stated, with a smirk. "We really can't have any more people running around, remembering anything."

She shook her head slowly. "I don't even know what you're talking about or why you're here. I don't get it." She bent a hand down to Lucky, who even now had turned back over and was cringing.

He stared at the dog and shrugged. "It's just another

mutt, so what do you care?"

"She's already been through a lot," Brittany snapped, "and, if you had any heart, you would care too."

"I don't give a shit about a dog," he stated coldly, "and I don't give a shit about you. I don't give a shit about this town or anything in it." He took a moment, looking around the space. "I'm here for something completely different."

"And what is that?" she asked, completely bewildered. "I have no idea what you could possibly want from me."

"Well, maybe nothing if you don't have what I want," he replied, "and that would make me very angry because I'm damn tired of searching all over the place and not finding it."

"What are you talking about?"

"I'm looking for a guy, one of the guys who lived in a house in the hurricane's path. The house is set pretty far back on his property, and he most definitely doesn't appreciate any visitors."

She winced. "Yeah, the spooky Gorman house."

He nodded. "Bingo. … You catch up fast. That would be a good name for it, and the old guy there was supposed to leave me something."

She frowned. "Well, go talk to him then," she cried out. "What are you doing here in my house?"

He glared at her. "Where is he? I need to know where he is."

"The old man? As far as I know he had surgery or something. I don't know any more than that. Maybe he died in the hurricane."

His glare deepened. "Don't give me that attitude. Which is it? He had surgery or he died?"

"How am I supposed to know?" She stared at him, wondering how she had gotten wrapped up in this. "I haven't seen him, and the townsfolk have always avoided that house like the plague."

"And that's probably smart. Gorman did his time, but he wasn't exactly one of the good guys," he shared, with a knowing smile.

She stared at him, her heart sinking. "Maybe he wasn't one of the good guys," she replied, "but, if he is dead, nobody can help you then. Presumably you've already gone to his house."

"I absolutely have," he declared, with a nod, "and it's a pretty depressing place. And now with the hurricane damage, it's pretty well destroyed too."

She nodded. "A lot of houses are like that around here."

He looked at her. "Did you lose a house?"

"My grandmother did. She had a house on that same block."

"I wondered why you kept coming back. Well, it's not exactly a town anybody wants to stay in, so I don't know why anybody would be upset over losing any home here. I suggest you take the money you're offered and run."

"I don't think it's that simple," she muttered, staring at him.

"It should be. It should be pretty-damn simple. I don't know why anybody would make it difficult," he said, glaring at her.

She let out her breath. "Look. I don't know what you want here."

"No, I'm sure you don't," he agreed, "but that's okay. It really is okay, and I don't have any ax to grind with you, *except* …"

It was the *except* that made her heart sink.

"Except that you've seen me."

"So what? What difference does it make if I've seen you?" she asked, staring at him. "I mean, I don't know your name. And it's not as if you're some celebrity. People won't come around here, wanting to take pictures of you or something."

He burst out laughing at that. "Yet I am a celebrity—but not in a way that you would care about."

She shook her head at the cryptic comment. "I don't know what you want from me, but this is my home, and you have no right to be here, so please leave."

"Oh so polite," he noted in a mocking tone, as he stepped closer. She stiffened and he nodded. "I really don't think you understand just what your situation is right now."

"No, I don't understand because I don't have anything to do with you. I don't know you, and I don't want to know you."

"Ah, now I'm heartbroken," he quipped, putting a hand against his heart, as he pulled out a gun.

"Oh no," she muttered, as she scrambled to her feet. Lucky scrambled to her feet too, obviously not enjoying the encounter with the stranger.

"And look at that," he said. "You've got the dog all upset too."

She spared a glance at Lucky, who was staring at the stranger, her lip curled. "She's upset because you're acting this way, and you're getting awfully close to her puppies."

He stopped, then stared down at them. "Shit, she survived the hurricane and had puppies? Aren't you just the luckiest?"

"Nothing wrong with her having puppies," Brittany declared, eyeing him. "It's just nature."

"Sure, but you know how it is around here. She could be

fodder for the gators," he shared, with a snort. "You should have just let them have her." Brittany gasped at him in shock, and he snorted. "You're just one of those animal-loving criminal-justice idiots," he declared, with a wave of his hand. "You don't have a clue how life works."

"Maybe not," she stated, "but I was doing pretty well until you came along." For whatever reason, that made him laugh, and he howled out loud with enjoyment. She stared at him, feeling weary. "It's not that funny."

Instantly his laughter stopped, and he looked at her and nodded slowly. "You're right. It isn't that funny. It's not funny at all." He pointed the gun straight at her.

She stared at him and shook her head. "Damn, not this again."

He frowned at her. "That's a pretty mellow attitude."

"No," she said, as she stared at the gun with loathing. "I've just come to really hate those things."

"Maybe, and maybe that's a good thing," he said. "But better to take something you're scared of and turn it into something you can utilize. The minute you're afraid of something," he noted in a lecturing tone, "it can be used against you."

She blinked at that. "Good to know."

"Not that you'll need to know it," he added, with that same smirk, "because no way I can let you live."

She stared at him. "Seriously? I don't even know who you are, and, if you hadn't showed up here, you would have been free to keep going and doing your own thing."

"Maybe, but the minute I get sloppy and somebody like you comes along and tells the cops about it, then my life becomes very difficult."

"You mentioned how you came to get something from

your friend. So go back to the Gorman house and get it," she cried out. "It's got nothing to do with me."

He just stared at her, then looked at the dog at her side and back at her. "You sound so sincere and believable, but sorry, no deal."

Just as he went to raise his weapon again, a huge roar surprised them. As the gunman spun to look at what was coming, she cried out, watching Kingston soar over the top of her fence and come down atop her intruder.

BARON BOLTED THROUGH the back door, just in time to see the gunman trying to shoot Kingston, who was trying to get at him. He called out to Kingston once, twice, then used an order common in the military to stand down.

The dog absolutely hated it but pulled back ever-so-slightly, glared at Baron for a second, then turned his attention to the man on the ground. Even now the intruder was trying to swing the gun forward, but Brittany kicked him in the ribs. He roared, then spun around with just enough energy to attack her, which set Kingston off yet again.

Baron now joined the fracas and pinned down the gunman, telling Brittany to go get him some zap straps or something to tie him up. Brittany bolted into the house, but Kingston wasn't leaving. He stayed right beside the intruder, growling at the man, just in case he dared to move.

"It's okay, buddy. It's okay," Baron said. "He won't try anything now. We've got him."

"Like fucking hell, you do," the gunman roared. "Ain't no way I'm letting that dog live. The minute I get up, I'm taking him out."

"You've got to get up first," Baron snapped, "and I'm not too worried about your doing that while Kingston's here."

Brittany returned almost immediately, with household zap straps. He nodded and zapped a couple together and pinned the man's arms in place, then worked on his legs. "Just in case you know a couple tricks to get out of these," he shared, "I'm doubling them up."

The angry gunman swore at him. "Yeah, I know how to get out of them."

"Don't bother," Baron snarled, while Kingston kept growling. "We won't make this easy on you."

"I don't give a shit if you make it easy or not," the intruder bellowed, his tone lethal and angry, "but I can guarantee I'm coming back after you."

Brittany finally asked Baron, "How did you know to come?"

Baron gave a nod to Kingston. "The War Dog sniffed out our prisoner coming here. You must have stopped by my truck, then come here. Kingston followed your scent."

"I'm gonna kill that dog," the prisoner yelled.

"I wonder about that," Baron noted, "since it seems to me that your buddy is the one you should be pissed at, … not me."

"And your fucking brother," he snapped.

At that, Baron froze. "Yeah. What did you do to my brother, asshole?"

"Wouldn't you like to know?" He sneered. "You'll have to figure it out on your own. I ain't fucking telling you shit."

"Then I won't tell you what we found either." The man stilled, and Baron knew he had him. "Yeah, you were looking for something, weren't you? Since Gorman and Brad seemed to be friendly, you searched my brother's house. Yet all Gorman and Brad had in common was a War Dog. So you kept going over to Gorman's place, but you never found anything, did you?"

"Old man Gorman is a fucking asshole. He was supposed to share all the goods we stole together back in the day. We agreed we would give it ten years before we cashed in. That son of a bitch had ten years, and he was supposed to keep it safe. Everybody in the gang knew our plans, and ten years went by. Then, all of a sudden, old man Gorman's supposedly got some mental illness. That old shit doesn't know where the stash is. People have come to his house and searched it, time and time again. Then he goes in for surgery, and I started wondering. … How is he paying for the damn surgery? He had the loot. What if he's using our money for that?"

"He was a war vet, as you well know. He had good military insurance that covered his VA hospital stays."

"Well, he shouldn't have nothing because nothing was honorable about him. He was nothing but a loser and a cheat, that son of a bitch. Where do you think we got the goods from?"

"You tell me."

"Gorman stole them. He got the information on one of those fancy foreign relations trips he ran with the military. Then one night, where supposedly all these people with big money were showing up, he let us all in, and we ended up stripping the place clean. We got tons of money and some gem collection too that was being stored at the time," he shared, with a sneer.

"So, you cleaned up lots of cash and jewelry?"

"Yeah, we did. Next thing I know, everything is on hold, just waiting for time to pass, for the investigation to cool, for the cops to lose interest. All these years, I've been just tinkering around, doing small-time jobs, waiting for the designated time to pass. Meanwhile, the gang is talking about it, what we'll do with our share, and we all know how much money is involved. It's worth more and more, and then, all of a sudden, Gorman starts losing his mind."

"Maybe he did lose it. Old age is like that, you know," Baron stated, as he stared down at his prisoner.

"Maybe, or maybe he stole it to pay for all this damn surgery. It was supposed to be our money."

"Well, he sure didn't put it into his house. He didn't dare, did he?"

"If he did any maintenance on his house, we would all know he'd been tapping into the money."

"But, as a war vet, he was eligible for medical."

"Maybe, but nobody else gets fucking medical in this world, so why the hell should Gorman? All he did was lie and cheat and steal—from the military."

"Maybe, but, if nobody knew that and if nobody was prepared to go to bat and to accuse him of something like that, then his medical would continue."

"Maybe," he sneered, "but you guys don't know shit when it comes to what goes on right under your nose."

"Oh, you might be surprised. Some of us do."

"Oh yeah, … here we go. You think you're better than everybody else? You're not any better than any of the rest of us."

"Then what happened to all the cash and the jewelry you stole?"

"I don't know. That's what I was looking for," he said,

frustration in his tone. "When the hurricane took the house out, I thought for sure it would be my chance to come and get the stash."

"What about your partner?"

"That double-crossing snake was here ahead of me. Matter of fact, he was here way ahead of me, and I didn't know it. After I got here, I found out he'd already been looking for days, but he hadn't told me that."

"Oh, he was just keeping that information for himself?" Brittany asked, pouring fuel on the fire from the sidelines.

"I'm not sure he's anything worth worrying about now," the prisoner muttered.

Baron held out a hand to her, and she took it, holding onto him tightly. "Yeah?" she replied. "Well, we've met him, and he seems to be pretty determined and persistent."

The gunman growled. "You don't know what the hell you're talking about. He's gone. What I'm talking about is millions in cash and in gold and gemstones over there."

Baron whistled at that. "Are you sure about the millions?"

"Hell, yes, I'm sure. I saw it."

"Wow, that's interesting," Baron said. "I remember hearing how a bunch of jewelry had been found during one of the military raids. They intercepted a huge cache of gold that was being moved on one of the missions, and it went missing."

"Yeah, it sure did. And Gorman set it up for us," the gunman confirmed. "Now about Gorman, … what kind of surgery is he having?"

Baron shrugged. "He has shrapnel in his back, as far as I know."

"Oh, that figures. It would be shrapnel in his back.

Serves him right, and that back-stabbing moron deserves all the pain he got. The guy is a loser, a flat-out loser."

"I'm not sure you have to worry about Gorman anymore either," Baron added.

"Why?"

"Because he passed away this morning."

At that, the gunman swore, loud and strong. "No way."

"Yeah, he did. The docs could only get part of the shrapnel, and he started bleeding heavily. He didn't make it through the night. They tried, but they could not save him."

"Hell." The gunman roared for a full minute, raging on, and then, tired and glum, he stared out into the distance, looking defeated. "That gold and the cash has to be somewhere."

"Something else I heard was how somebody had reported on the sly about where and how the missing gold and jewels were found," Baron shared, "and it was taken back into military custody about, … let me think, … maybe five years later."

"No way!" the gunman shouted, twisting to try and look up at him. "What the fuck are you saying? How the hell—"

"Think about it."

"You are saying he …" The intruder frowned.

At that, Baron nodded. "Yes."

"He was a goddamn snitch? But how the hell would you know about it?"

"It's just the work I'm in, you know? I hear rumors."

"Yeah? Rumors don't mean shit."

"I think Gorman probably turned it in, saying he came across some people trying to sell the gold, trying to launder the cash. That's the story I heard."

The guy just stared at him. "Gorman wouldn't do that."

"He might have, if he had second thoughts."

"No, no, he wouldn't. … He wouldn't dare. … It was *our* money, and he knew it. Damn it. He was the one who stole it in the first place."

"If he stole it," Brittany suggested, as she stood up and walked closer, "then maybe Gorman decided it was up to him to return it to the rightful owners."

"Who is the rightful owner in a war?" the intruder asked, with a laugh. "That's why it was so fucking perfect."

"Ah, right, … untraceable gold and all that cash."

"It had been moved into Gorman's house for safekeeping, and all these supposed guards were around, but our gang was part of the guards, so we were some of the few people able to move it out. It was perfect, and nobody even knew. Hell, I didn't connect all the dots until we'd moved it here. It was the perfect place …"

"You had it, but that didn't mean you got to keep it," Brittany pointed out. "So what about your partner? The one who beat you here."

He just shrugged.

"What? Did you pop him too?" she asked.

He glared at her and snapped, "I wasn't sharing any more than I had to."

"Right, so once again, greed is the whole reason your partnership blew up."

"Not greed," he clarified. "There were four of us, and we were called the Galloway gang. One obviously has just passed away," he noted, glaring at Baron, "while two of us were here and were doing just fine. At least we would have been, if we could have found the damn stash. I still don't know where Gorman could have kept it. All I know is, it's not at his house any longer so maybe the military did get it."

"Depending on the physical size of the stash, safe deposit boxes make some sense, if you think about it."

"Yeah, but Gorman didn't have one. We checked."

"You checked every name that he had, that he could have possibly used?" Baron asked.

The gunman eyed him and nodded. "We had one storage locker in all our names," he shared, "so it shouldn't have been an issue. The plan was to move the stash from Gorman's house to the locker, before he retired from the military. We just had to get the right people on the security detail."

"Yet I'm telling you that somebody turned in a parcel of gold at some point, and it's been a bit ago."

"When you say a bit ago, how long exactly?"

Baron shrugged. "As I told you earlier, about five years after it was stolen. I'm not exactly privy to the inside story, but I could probably find out."

Brittany frowned, listening intently, as she sat on the other side of Kingston, keeping him calm.

"If Gorman turned it in," the gunman replied, now swearing, "that would be a shitty move for the rest of us."

"It might be shitty for you," Baron noted, looking at him, "but maybe the authorities were looking at in a whole different light."

"What are you talking about?"

"Because maybe the fourth man in your group," Baron suggested calmly, "maybe he turned on you."

"I haven't heard from him. I sent him a message that we were coming to look for our stash, that the place had gone down in a hurricane, and that old man Gorman was missing."

"Maybe the fourth man came to make his claim. Maybe

he was already here ahead of you and your partner," Brittany suggested.

The gunman just glared at her. Baron looked over at her and shook his head slightly. Frowning, she snapped her lips shut.

"What the hell is it that I don't know," the gunman asked, slowly catching on.

"*One* of the things that you don't know is that the fourth man in your group was a plant," Baron shared. "Did you ever see him?"

"No, I never saw him. Everything was done in secret."

"Right, so you see? That's part of the problem. He was a plant, and you don't know who it was. So he couldn't let everybody know what really happened. Plus old man Gorman managed to hang on to his medical and his pension because he agreed to testify, if you were ever found. Apparently you guys weren't too interested in showing up."

"We agreed to have no contact for ten years."

"Exactly, and now ten years have gone by. Gorman's not here with us any longer," Baron pointed out, "and it looks like you and the buddy you already killed were the only ones left to the Galloway gang—plus the other guy, the plant."

"What do you mean, he was a plant?"

"He knew all about the heist, and he reported it to the authorities beforehand," Baron replied.

"How the hell would you know that?" Instantly angry all over again, the gunman twisted in front of him.

Baron glanced over at Brittany, who was also staring at him with growing wonder. Baron shrugged. "Because I'm that guy."

CHAPTER 13

B RITTANY SAT BACK on her haunches and stared at him. He looked over at her with half a smile. "I was in intelligence," he added.

She nodded. "Of course you were." She shook her head. "Did your brother know?"

"To some degree. Not a whole lot of it, but he knew bits and pieces."

She looked down at the guy they had trussed up. "Did Brad know about this group, this Galloway gang?"

"He knew of the possibility of the gang's return to get their stolen goods," Baron shared, "and I forewarned him, as much as I could. We knew it was only a matter of time before the gang came looking. But the gang didn't know about that. These guys just knew that Brad and old man Gorman seemed to talk to each other a lot. Little did they know it was about the War Dog."

"So—"

"Yeah, I came home periodically over the past decade, always under some pretense. The recent hurricane gave me an opportunity too, and, no, I'm not part of the investigation anymore," he admitted, raising his hands, "and neither was my brother. He shouldn't have gone looking, and I don't know for sure that he did. I do know that he would have been more worried about the animals than the gold or the cash."

"That was your brother," grumbled the gunman. "What an idiot."

"He wasn't an idiot," Baron snapped, cuffing him sharply on his head. "He was a good man who found value in things other than money."

"Then he must be a man who had money because, without it, our world is pretty rough," the gunman snapped right back. "And somebody like you doesn't know the meaning of *rough*."

She stared down at him. "You don't know anything about him," she stated, as she walked several steps away and bent down to hug Lucky.

"How is she?" Baron asked.

Something in his tone got her attention, and she looked over at him and gave him a reassuring smile. "She's fine." Thinking about what he'd revealed in this conversation, she asked, "You were the young punk they had as part of the Galloway gang, right?"

He nodded. "I was the one they planned to shoot in the back, just using me as a way to get intel and afterward to toss me away. Then they decided to keep me as part of the gang."

"We should have shot you dead at the beginning," the angry gunman snapped.

"Maybe so," Baron muttered. "Maybe you should have."

BARON PULLED OUT his phone and made a call he didn't think he would ever make in his lifetime. When the commander answered the line, Baron introduced himself.

"You better have a good goddamn reason for calling

me," he replied, his tone clipped and impatient.

"I do," he replied, then quickly explained.

Immediately the hard tone switched to a loud cheer in his ear. "Now that's a call I've been waiting for," he declared. "I'll get men coming your way right now."

"Good, but get here before the cops do because they'll want this guy too," Baron shared. "I'm also trying to figure out if he had anything to do with my brother's death."

"He may well have, particularly if Brad knew anything."

"Brad didn't know anything, but I still think there's a damn-good chance this guy may have helped him on his way."

"We'll get it out of him."

"I'm not sure he's military though, so he might not be your jurisdiction."

"He is. He's our mess because he was once one of us. He went out on a dishonorable discharge, so don't worry about it. He'll be coming back for a full accounting."

And, with that, Baron's phone went dead. He looked down at the gunman, who stared at him, wild-eyed. "I guess you won't like the next part of your life."

"No, I sure as fucking hell won't," he yelled, his gaze searching the area, frantic, looking for an escape.

"Don't bother," Baron said, "and don't forget we've got Kingston on you as well. You'll be alive if the military takes you, but, if it's up to Kingston, … he's ready to rip you apart."

"I don't give a crap about that dog," he grumbled, "and I'll kill the fucking thing if I ever get a chance."

"Like you did my brother?"

He turned, looked at him, and snarled. "As much as I would like to say that I did kill your brother, I didn't. I had stopped to talk to him and ended up letting out a bunch of the dogs, but people started coming, and I thought, … fuck it, I'm leaving," he said, "and that piece of shit dog was there too. When I turned to look back he was already in the river and it was too late to do anything."

At that, Kingston growled deep in the back of his throat. When the man growled right back, Kingston made one snap, and the man jumped back. "Shit, I hate these fucking things."

"You may hate them," Baron replied, "but they serve a great purpose, particularly when it comes to assholes like you."

"Maybe so"—he glared at him—"and, if I get loose, you know where I'm coming."

"I don't have to worry about you getting free, and I didn't call the regular military or the regular police for that matter," he shared, with a smile in his direction. "That's a call I've been hoping to make for a very long time."

"Yeah? You probably came snooping around here every time you visited your brother, didn't you?"

"I sure did. I did, indeed." Baron grinned. "And now you've given me closure that I hadn't expected either. I'm glad to know you didn't kill my brother. He did have a heart condition that none of us ever could quite understand. His life was bound to be cut short at some point, and you might have scared him into it, but—"

"*Nah*, he was pretty upset over the dogs and the animals and all the rest of that crap. I watched him scurry around, trying to collect all the animals he could. What a fucking miserable piece of shit."

"Brad met his maker in good graces," Baron declared. "You, on the other hand, won't be quite so lucky."

"Speak for yourself," he grumbled. "It's not like they'll shoot me." His eyes opened wide. "Wait. Who did you call?"

Baron grinned broadly. "You'll have to wait and find out."

"Guantanamo Bay? As another 'forever prisoner'? You can't do that. You can't drop me there. You can't hide me away, then forget about me."

"Oh, they could pop you into a couple different prisons and throw away the key. You know there won't be a trial. There won't be anything. You'll just disappear from the face of the earth, and nobody will even notice."

"No, no, no, they can't do that."

"Why not?" he asked with interest, as he watched him. "I'm sure you know other guys who had the exact same thing happen to them."

The man started to panic. "You don't understand."

"I do understand," Baron corrected, "and, just in case you have any doubts about who I am, I remember your code name too. *Bennie.*"

The man stared at him, frowning, trying to see Baron's younger self. "No, no, no. It can't be you. You were just a fucking ass piece of shit."

"Yeah, a fucking ass piece of shit partner, who you wanted taken down, instead of splitting the payout with. You just didn't know who I was."

"But I heard you got hurt in some accident."

"Yeah, he did," Brittany interjected, "but he's back on top again, so don't you worry about him."

"It really is you, isn't it?" the gunman asked, staring at him.

"Yeah, it really is."

"Shit, I guess I didn't really know anybody involved on

that job."

"It was a pretty risky job in the first place," Baron pointed out, "but the military knew. They knew about it from the start, which is why I was even there."

"But we saw the gold, the stones. We—"

"Yeah, but it wasn't real gold, not genuine gemstones either," Baron shared, with a knowing smile. "It was a setup right from the start."

At that, Bennie ranted and raved. He was still ranting, raving, and practically frothing at the mouth over it, when a call came from the front door.

Baron looked over at Brittany and asked, "Could you go get them, please?"

Brittany raced to the front door but not Kingston. Kingston stayed right beside Baron.

When two men in black suits stepped into the backyard, they looked over at Baron. After one handed him an ID, Baron nodded. "Here's your prisoner."

They scooped him up, patted him down, making sure he had no more weapons, then replaced the zap straps with handcuffs and leg irons. Giving both of them a quick nod, one tipped his hat to Brittany. "Ma'am." And, with that, they were gone.

Baron settled on the grassy spot, taking the pressure off his ankle, swearing at the joint once again, knowing he would have to speak to Kat about it. Then his phone rang.

"So," Badger began casually, "I just got an interesting phone call."

"Yeah, I wanted to follow up on that," Baron replied. "It's all good. They just picked him up."

"Seems that you probably got closure on quite a bit then. What about your brother?"

"Well, Bennie didn't kill Brad, so, for that, I'm very grateful."

"Yes, I would think so. And Kingston?"

"Kingston has broken a lot of hearts," he replied, turning to see Brittany with her arms around the War Dog, hugging him tight. "He's also found a girlfriend."

"A girlfriend," Badger repeated, with a chuckle. "Now that's interesting."

"She's one of the dogs my brother had. She'd been abused and was in pretty rough shape but proceeded to have puppies out in the rubble after the hurricane hit, after my brother died. Nobody knew what the hell had happened to her, and that's where Kingston was the whole time, protecting her."

"Ah, now who doesn't like a really good love story," Badger said, chuckling.

"I don't know how much of a love story it is," Baron stated, as he walked over to where Brittany now hugged both dogs, "but it's definitely good to see all the changes around here."

"You think you'll be okay there now?"

"Yeah, I do," he stated. "I'll give you a full report in a little bit, but right now—"

"It's all good," Badger noted. "I'll need a report of course, but, as long as Kingston's fine, and you're fine, we're good to go for now. We do have to find a solution for the War Dog's long-term care going forward though." Pausing, he waited, then added, "Unless of course you're looking to keep him."

Baron snorted. "Do you blindside all your guys that way?"

"Don't have to. Most of the time, as you may have

guessed, they're jumping at the chance to keep these War Dogs."

"I don't know what I'm doing just now," Baron admitted. "Is it true that Kingston's owner, old man Gorman, is dead?"

"Yes, he didn't survive the surgery," Badger confirmed, "so the War Dog's future care is definitely up in the air, but I have the authority to appoint a new owner."

"Right," Baron said, with a grin. "I suppose that, given the circumstances, I could probably keep him."

"Okay then." With a note of laughter in his tone, Badger added, "So what will you do with his girlfriend? And how many puppies did she have?"

"Six," he replied, with a groan.

"Well, there you go. So, if nothing else, for the next little bit, you've got puppies to look after. I reckon that makes you a K9 nursemaid."

"Oh, *great*. Thank you so much for that flattering job title."

"You're welcome. We'll talk in a bit." And, with that, Badger rang off.

"Did I hear him say something about a K9 nursemaid?" Brittany giggled, her hands over her mouth.

He walked over, scooped her into his arms, wincing as the leg complained. Yet he hugged her and then set her back down gently again. He lowered his head and gave her a light kiss on the lips. "You did, but I'm not answering to that job title."

"I think it's great," she declared, still laughing.

He shook his head, then walked over to Lucky and asked, "How are you doing, girl? You're okay, and it will be all fine now." He looked back at Brittany. "How are you holding up?"

"Better now," she said. "I have to admit you came into my life alongside that hurricane and stirred it up completely. I'm not sure it'll ever be the same again."

"Does it need to be the same again, or are you okay to have something completely different?"

"Completely different works," she confirmed with a smile, as she walked closer. "Are we still up for dinner on Friday?"

"I think we should have dinner Friday, and maybe Saturday, Sunday, and Monday too. I don't know about you, but I'm good to fill up every day of your week."

Her eyes widened, and she wrapped her arms around him. "I don't think I've had a nicer invitation."

He leaned over, kissed her gently, and added, "I'm glad to hear that. It's been a pretty rough couple days."

"It has." She hesitated, then looked at him. "Will you be okay if, you know …" Then her voice dropped off.

"There you go again," he said. "Letting your words drop off midsentence."

She smiled. "Well, that's just one of the things you'll have to get used to."

"Or you'll learn to be so comfortable in your own skin that you'll know you can say exactly what you need to say." Her eyes widened, and he nodded. "That happens when, deep down, you don't think that whatever you need to say will be well received, but you can always tell me anything."

She smiled. "I'm glad to hear that," she muttered, "because I'm not sure that's something I've ever really had."

"Probably not," he agreed, with a smile. "Maybe with your grandmother, maybe not, but she's old school, and sometimes it's harder for old school to deal with today's issues."

"She's definitely old school, but she's also pretty modern." She looked up at him. "Will you live in your brother's house?"

He nodded. "Yeah, and it's only a few blocks from yours."

"Well, it's only a few blocks from where my grandma's house was," she clarified, with a sigh. "I'm a little farther away than that."

"Not enough to count," he stated, "and, on a good day, it will make for a great walk. Besides, I suspect we'll be spending a lot of time at my house."

"Oh, will we? And why is that?" she asked, with an eye roll.

"Because it's bigger, and the dogs will be there, and it's got a big yard for a family."

Her eyes widened. "Whoa, whoa, whoa. I don't know what you're talking about there," she said, raising her hands animatedly. "Let's just slow down there, soldier."

He smiled. "Let me clarify. It's big enough for a puppy family."

She blinked and collapsed into laughter. "Oh my gosh, being around you is like being on a damn roller coaster. I never quite know what you'll say next."

"And that's okay too," he said. "I wouldn't want you to get too complacent."

"Well, a little complacent would be nice," she muttered, as she smiled up at him.

"Besides, it really does have a nice family-size yard."

She shook her head. "That is a discussion for later, definitely not today."

"Ah," he replied, as he glanced down at her, "but you are

interested in the discussion, I hope."

She sighed. "Maybe."

"Nope, no maybes about it," he declared, as he pulled her into his arms and held her close, "but I know it's fast."

"It's not just fast. It's stupidly crazy fast."

"Okay, so I know it's stupidly crazy fast," he confirmed, still holding her, "and I'm definitely not saying that's where we have to end up, but I am saying that's a place I would really like to go."

She wrapped her arms around him and whispered, "You know something? I wouldn't mind that either."

"So, why don't we both go on this relationship journey and just see how we come out?"

"Sounds good to me," she replied, as she went up on her toes and kissed him. "But I don't know if I'll be a decent mother or not."

"And I don't know if I'll be a decent father," he added, looking at her.

They both turned, looked at Lucky, and Brittany smiled. "I guess when it comes to parenting, we've got a chance to try it out on the dogs first."

He chuckled. "If you're around me, you'll need to handle lots of dogs," he shared. "I'm not sure what I'll do with my life, outside of getting my brother's will sorted and ..." His voice dropped. "I found out something else that my mother and my brother were keeping from me." Then he told her about his mother's health.

Tears filled Brittany's eyes, and she whispered, "I'm so sorry."

"Well, at least I know now and can make the best of whatever time we have," he noted, "and the same goes for your grandmother."

"Right," Brittany agreed. "So, we can appreciate the people we have in our lives, while we work on building our own. Got it." She slipped her hand in his and added, "You know something?"

"What?" he asked, as he looked at the dogs and back at her.

"I think I could use a nap."

"A nap?" he asked unsurely.

She winked at him. "Yes, and how about now?"

He frowned and asked, "Are you sure? We would have to leave all the animals on their own."

"Nope, we can just leave the door open." He stared at her, and she shrugged. "Now that all the trouble is over with."

"What about the gunman's partner?" he asked. "Have you forgotten that?"

"Nope. I'm pretty sure Bennie took out that guy."

He nodded. "I'm pretty sure he did too. We just need to figure out where and get that confirmed."

"No," she disagreed, placing a finger against his lips. "Remember how you're not active military anymore? You've done what they really needed you to do, and now you're off the hook." She stepped inside and added, "Besides, even if you were to have a look, you can't go right now."

"Really, and why's that?" he asked, as he followed her inside.

"Because of that *nap*," she repeated, with a big grin, "one we definitely need." Then she raced up to her bedroom, and he followed closely behind.

CHAPTER 14

BRITTANY RACED INTO her bedroom, laughing and giggling. She wasn't even sure how she ended up as the seducer this time, but she was damn glad she did. She flung herself onto her bed, her arms and legs akimbo, and when he came through the bedroom door just shaking his head, she was posing. "What's the matter, am I scary?"

"You're damn scary," he replied, with a big grin on his face, "but I think I can handle it."

"In that case," she teased, as she opened her arms wide, "get down here."

"Oh, will you be gentle with me?" he asked in mock horror. "What if I haven't done this in a while?"

"That'll make two of us." He climbed onto the bed beside her, one eyebrow raised. She nodded. "Not since the breakup at my wedding."

"I'm sorry," he muttered.

She shrugged. "No, it's okay. I just decided that I didn't like what was going on in my world and the people I was hanging out with. I didn't want to have sex, just for the sake of sex. I didn't care for it on those terms. For me, it always needed to be about my heart."

"Well, I'm glad that something to do with your heart includes me," he whispered, as he rolled over onto his back and pulled her with him.

She smiled down at him. "Will we really have a relationship with all these dogs and puppies?"

"Why not?" he asked. "I think your life was a little empty and a little safe before, wasn't it?"

She winced. "Wow, it didn't take you very long to pick up on that."

He smiled. "It didn't take long to pick up on it because I understood it. Once you've been hurt, it's hard to step out of that safe comfort zone you create for yourself, and it's hard to go into a place where you're opening yourself back up again."

"That's one of the reasons I didn't have another relationship," she admitted. "I didn't feel as if I could trust my own judgment."

He raised up and kissed her. "Well, I hope you consider your judgment decent now."

"Oh, maybe," she teased, chuckling, "but you still must prove it to me."

"We don't have to prove anything," he said, with a headshake.

She nodded. "You're right. I'm a little rusty."

"No," he countered, "you're not rusty at all. You're coming from the heart, and you're a little nervous, but I don't want you scared."

"I'm not scared of you," she stated, and then shook her head. "It's just the whole *opening myself up again*, which is supposed to be so easy."

"Who said that?" he asked her. "I don't think anything is easy about opening yourself up because it makes you vulnerable."

She nodded. "That's not an easy place to be."

"But, with you, somehow it feels normal, and it feels

right."

She smiled. "I'm not in any way afraid of you."

"Good," he whispered.

"So, you really worked undercover?"

"Let's just say that I've been involved in this for a very long time, and certain people realized where I was from. So, considering that they still wanted to pick up the other players involved in this theft, it was something I was asked to look into."

She rolled her eyes. "I think you forgot to mention that part to me."

"I didn't make a whole lot of noise when I came to town, did I? I was a local, in a sense. So nobody raised any suspicions. I've been around here for years," he added, "and I have seen you around."

"Ah, but you just weren't interested in me."

"It wasn't that I wasn't interested in you. I wasn't interested in anything permanent. Then I got injured, and I figured nobody would want me, at least for a while there," he shared. "Over time I've gotten to the point where it was like my injury didn't matter. My injury didn't change who I was. I would go forward with my life, and, if I could solve this investigation, while spending time with my family, then it was all good."

"I'm so sorry about your brother."

"Me too," he muttered, with a sigh. "But he died doing what he loved, and I'm very grateful that, although he may have been pushed into the heart attack, the Galloway gang didn't kill him."

"You're right about that, and he may well have been pushed into a heart attack. That Bennie guy and his partner were pretty damn scary." He smiled, nodding. "But then again," she added, tapping him on the chin, "so are you. I think we should go for a swim."

He looked at her. "So a swim first, then a nap?"

She giggled.

"And where on earth will we go for a swim?"

"I know a little private spot."

He nodded. "In that case, let's go." She hesitated, and he raised an eyebrow.

"What about your leg?"

"What about it?" he asked and then shrugged. "Depending on how hard it is to get to your private spot, my leg isn't waterproof. I'm supposed to be getting a model that would allow me that, but it isn't ready yet," he shared, "so I'll find a way to make it work."

"But then you would only have one leg."

"Hell, I only have one whole leg now," he pointed out in exasperation, "and it's not the end of the world. This is all about what I can do, not what I might do."

She smiled and nodded. "In that case, let's go. A dock is right along the edge."

"Perfect," he replied. "I can leave my prosthetic on the dock, and we can go for a swim."

She hopped off the bed and raced to get a bathing suit. Then she stopped and turned to look at him. "We don't really need a bathing suit, but I'll bring one ... just in case."

"You bring one just in case," he agreed, "and I'll go with my shorts because I don't have one."

"Okay," she murmured. Then she stepped into her bathroom and changed into her bathing suit and a cover-up. Then, laughing like crazy, they headed downstairs. She looked at the dogs, and he patted Kingston.

Baron shrugged. "If we take one, we would have to take

all of them."

"Fine, we're leaving them all behind then," she decided. "This is just for us."

In the truck, she gave him directions on how to get to the lake, and as they pulled into a private driveway, he asked, "Whose place is this?"

She looked over at him and smiled. "It's mine."

His eyebrows shot up. "Seriously?"

"Yes."

"What waterway is this?" She explained it to him, and he nodded. "So, this is fresh water?"

"Yes, it's not so much a lake as a tributary, but I own the land. I always thought I would build here someday."

"Well, you've got one hell of a view," he noted, as he got out and looked around. The ocean was right there. "Now look who has secrets."

She nodded. "I bought it a long time ago, after my engagement broke up. We had dated a while and even been engaged for a while, so I'd been saving for a place. Then I realized just how fickle life was, so I decided to create it for myself."

"I like that," he said, turning to smile at her. "It's a great idea."

She shrugged. "It's something I've always wanted to do."

"I can definitely get behind your dreams, so don't let others, not even me, talk you out of it."

She nodded. "That's why I'm telling you," she declared, with a smile. "You have plans, and you're capable of making plans happen, and I like that."

He smiled. "So, … down to the dock then?"

She nodded and led the way. The ground was a little bit on the rough side, but, as they reached the dock, it was long and wide. "I've been meaning to come and check on the state of the dock anyway," she shared. "It's a little more protected here, and I'm glad to see it's completely unscathed by the hurricane." She sat here for a moment, her eyelids closed, her face turned up to the sun.

His tone, thick and soft, he whispered, "Beautiful."

She turned and looked at him, then realized he was staring at her. She smiled. "Not quite as beautiful as Mother Nature," she conceded, with a smile. "It truly is beautiful here."

"And you," he stated firmly, "are stunning. The beauty that starts from the inside is always the best kind on the outside, and don't you ever forget it."

He quickly shucked off his shirt and then his jeans. He looked at her and asked, "Are you okay that it's boxers?"

"I'm totally okay that it's boxers," she said, with a laugh.

She watched with interest as he slowly took off his prosthetic and noted that he had most of his leg, including the knee and some shin beyond that. "Can you walk like that?"

He nodded. "I can put weight on it but emergencies only. Still it does give me an option, if I have to."

"That sounds like something you are managing then."

"It is what it is," he replied, with a smile at her direction. "I'm very much … think of it this way. You make do with what you've got and live with the rest."

"I like that too," she murmured, as she studied him. "I sure hope you know how to swim." And, with that, she dropped her cover-up and made a running jump and dove off the end of the peer. He followed suit from where he stood on the deck, jumping into the water, then he quickly swam up to where she was.

"I guess if you were in the military, you probably know

how to swim."

"I do know how to swim," he confirmed, with a cheeky grin, "even with only one leg."

"Oh my, I didn't even think of that."

"And you don't need to think of it either," he stated firmly. "It's amazing what we can do when we put our minds to it."

She looped her arms around his neck. "But can you tread water and hug me?"

He pulled her in for a deep soul-searing kiss and whispered, "Of course I can."

And when she realized that he was standing in the water and holding her close, she burst out laughing. "I didn't realize it was so shallow right here."

"It is." He grinned, as he looked around. "How private is it here?"

"Very private. It's one of the things I love about it."

"I had no idea this was here."

"Well, it is," she murmured, "and it's definitely a place where I want to spend more time."

"Absolutely," he murmured, as he looked around. "It's beautiful, and you are blessed to have it."

"I haven't even told my grandmother about it."

He looked at her. "Why not?"

"I don't know," she admitted, pulling back her hair. "I think because … it was just after being left at the altar, and I felt as if everybody knew so much about me, with the eating disorder thing too. So it just seemed like nothing in my life was private," she explained. "This was something I could keep just for me."

"You don't need to feel guilty about it," he murmured. "Your grandmother would be happy for you."

"I know. She definitely would be. I think it was just … I don't know. I think I just needed something that was just mine."

"And you've got it," he said, as he kissed her again.

She threw her arms around him and murmured, "It's a perfect place."

"It is. Maybe you should build yourself a house out here. Meanwhile, your grandmother stays with Camille for the short term, as you find out what retirement home options are out there. Wait to see how much the insurance company will give you for your grandma's house. Even if the house is a goner, your grandmother could still take the insurance payout and then sell the land, setting that aside for the retirement home. For that matter, you could rent or buy an old doublewide trailer and set it on the property specifically for your grandmother. That is, if the zoning laws allow for it. Then there is always the option that your grandmother lives with you at your current place for a bit, before you build your new house. Then you live there and let Grandma live in your old house, maybe paying you some nominal rent." When her eyes grew huge, he added, "Just suggestions. Nothing that you have to do. Certainly nothing you must decide right now. After all, we've got swimming to do. Plus that nap you mentioned earlier."

"I'm game, as long as you don't drown me," she said, laughing.

It wasn't very long before she had her arms and legs wrapped around him, and she realized that they still had too many clothes on. She separated herself from him and quickly pulled off her bathing suit, only to find that it was already three-quarters off. She raised one eyebrow and shared in a sassy tone, "I see you were working on something here."

"I was," he admitted, "but you're making life a lot easier for me."

She shook her head as she tossed it onto the dock, and then his boxers hit the dock right beside her top. She laughed and swam back to him.

He quickly caught her in his arms and held her against him, skin to skin, chest to chest, hips to hips, tightly against him, his hands wrapping all the way around and holding her firmly. "I wasn't expecting this," he murmured. "It wasn't even on my radar."

"Nor on mine," she muttered, as she stroked his face.

"I'm really glad that sometimes good things happen to good people."

"Your brother was one of those good people."

"Well, I hope you never did this with him," he shared in mock distress.

She burst out in peals of laughter. "No, I never did," she murmured, "but he was still good people."

"He was, and I know he's happy for us."

With that, he lowered his head and started dropping kisses across her face and around her wet hair. She tilted her head up higher, giving him better access. He shifted until she wrapped her arms around his neck and her legs around his waist, while he stood deep in the lake water.

"My God," she whispered, when she finally came up for air after his kisses. "I can't believe how freeing it is to be out here like this."

"Most people don't do the nudist thing," he murmured, his lips busy against her throat.

"I've never done it before either," she whispered, "but it's definitely a unique experience."

"As long as we're private and not intruding on anybody

else's world," he said, "I'm all for it." Then he lowered his head again, kissing her deeply. When they came up for air again, she was gasping, shivering in his arms. "Are you cold?" he asked, his tone sharp and concerned.

"No," she whispered, "just needy."

He smiled. "I think I can take care of that."

Before she realized it, he slid deep inside her and held her tight, pinned hip to hip. She shuddered at his possession, the water, the silky sensation, the complete freedom, and damn if her body didn't erupt in joy. He held her through it all and then slowly began to move.

She had to laugh at the splashing of the water up and around both of them. Finally she tightened her hips against his and suggested, "You stay still, and I'll move."

And, with that, she pumped against him, hard and deep, until he groaned and grabbed her hips, holding her tight and grinding up against her. When he exploded, it sent off tremors again, as a second orgasm ripped through her.

She moaned softly as he just held on to her. "Oh my God," she muttered, "why did I wait for so long?"

His laughter rippled across the lake. "I don't know," he whispered, "but I can't say I'm against it. It's nice to know you were waiting for me."

"Well, I didn't know I was waiting for you," she corrected. "But now that I do know, I'm really happy it was you." He blinked at that, and she laughed. "Don't worry about it. I was just working my way through that preamble."

He smiled. "As long as you worked your way through it, … I'm good." He slowly walked her back toward the dock. "I don't think I've ever done that before," Baron shared.

She nodded. "I know I haven't."

"It was great," he added, "and I've spent a lot of time in the water."

She smiled. "Sounds like a new one for both of us."

He got her back to the dock and then settled down on it, drying out in the warm sunshine. She stretched out beside him, on the warm decking. "It is absolutely beautiful here," she murmured.

"It sounds like this is really where your heart is."

"In a way it is," she said. "I mean, I love being down at grandma's house too, but it was always so exposed, and mine is too. It works, but I've always wanted something a little more private."

"You found it," he declared, "and this is truly a gift for you."

She reached out her hand, and, with their fingers laced together, he remained stretched out beside her. She asked him, "Are you okay to not have your prosthetic on?"

"I am," he muttered. "For some people it becomes something they can't handle or are uncomfortable with," he explained, "but I worked hard to find a level of comfort with mine. I want to be capable and independent, both with and without it." Now that he was mostly dried off, he put on his boxers and his shirt. He kept his prosthetic and his pants nearby.

She rolled her head to the side, loving the strong cast to his features, and that whole *can do, will do, take charge* attitude. "And you'll keep Kingston?" she asked, now donning her bathing suit again.

He grinned and turned to her and asked, "What do you think?"

She nodded. "I think you'll keep Kingston, and you'll keep Lucky, and, if we aren't careful, you'll also keep the puppies."

He burst out laughing at that. "I don't know yet. We'll see. Maybe we'll try to find good homes for the puppies, when it's time. Lucky needs to heal first, but, when she is able, we'll get her fixed, then see if she has any training. If not, I'll have somebody I can work with right away." He sighed. "This is a perfect end to a very long week."

"I couldn't agree more," she whispered, once more beside him.

He settled on the dock again, rolled his head back, stared up at the sun, and closed his eyelids, their fingers linked again.

"Personally I'm okay if this is the start of the rest of my life."

"It absolutely is," he confirmed, "and that's what todays always are. Tomorrows never come, and, every time you wake up, it's the start of a whole new wave of what you want."

"All I want is you."

"Sounds good to me," he whispered, "because all I want is you."

Then, closing their eyes, they both napped in the sun, happy and content, knowing they had started something good for the both of them.

K AT FROWNED AT Badger. "Are you telling me that
Baron was working undercover the whole time?"

He nodded.

"That sneaky little bastard."

"I assumed you knew that. When you mentioned his
name, I knew it was in some document in that file of yours,"
he noted, "and I had to make a few phone calls to figure out
what was going on. It's one of the reasons I kept tabs on
Baron a little more closely."

"And he solved his undercover case too, as well as finding Kingston," she said. "That's amazing."

"Isn't it? I know I'm really happy with it."

"So you should be," she stated. "This is huge."

"And now what?" he asked.

"I have only one more file on the table. Well, one more
right now, but I'm not sure it'll be the end though."

"Maybe not," Badger agreed, "but we'll take it one at a
time. Tell me about this one."

"Believe it or not, it's back to Alaska again."

He stared at her and shook his head. "How much will
the flight cost?"

"I had to get a little cagey to cut that down, so I have a
client already in Alaska, who would be a good fit."

He stared at her, his eyebrow shooting up. "My God, are

you so well-known now that we have people everywhere?"

"Maybe," she quipped, with a smile. "I haven't talked to him about it and don't know if it's something he's interested in, but he was a K9 trainer in the military for quite a few years. He did lose several of his best friends in the process and ended up injured in an accident not long afterward. So maybe, just maybe …"

"And what's his name?"

"Walton."

Badger's eyebrow shot up again. "You do understand that I know him, right?"

"Of course," she replied. "You know everybody. Maybe not everybody, but you do know a lot of people. And it makes sense that you would know this one. … Plus we still have Timber to deal with."

Badger's frown was immediate.

She nodded. "I know," she said, "but he's heading into his own place. We need to give him as much help as we can."

"I don't have a problem with that, but …" His voice trailed off, as he stared into the distance, but he finally nodded. "I know that Timber's time is coming, but I also know that a big mystery is in the back of his world too. Maybe we need to help him with that."

"As soon as he gets set up and settled."

"I'm not sure he's quite ready for that, so let's figure it out as we go."

She added, "I want to help him too."

"You do know that you can't help everyone, right?"

"I know that," she said, rolling her eyes as she got up. Then she neared Badger and looped her arms around him, giving him a big hug. "But I still want to try to help everyone who crosses my path." She kissed him on the cheek and turned to walk away.

He watched the woman of his life, the woman of his heart, and realized again just how damn special she was. She stopped at the doorway, smiled back at him, and added, "Besides, I have a really big heart and room for a lot more, … lots and lots more."

This concludes Book 25 of The K9 Files: Baron.
Read about Walton: The K9 Files, Book 26

The K9 Files: Walton (Book #26)

Welcome to the all new K9 Files series reconnecting readers with the unforgettable men from SEALs of Steel in a new series of action packed, page turning romantic suspense that fans have come to expect from USA TODAY Bestselling author Dale Mayer. Pssst… you'll meet other favorite characters from SEALs of Honor and Heroes for Hire too!

Walton Headly enjoys getting out and being as active as he can be, given his missing leg. However, playing soccer now is hard to adapt to, compared to playing soccer before his injury. He has been in rehab for a long time and now reaches a need to do more. Searching for a missing War Dog sounds like a great way to ease back into a working life.

Chelsea Brown, a physical therapist, had helped get Walton back on his feet. He is one hell of a man but is struggling after that last soccer game. Her invitation to contact her older brother at his hunting lodge for any information on the missing War Dog yields more than expected. Together they head north to visit her brother and to check out the dog, who has just arrived with the new guests.

Finding out the guests are not ordinary hunters—and the dog is not an ordinary dog—causes conflict from the first meet. And goes steadily downhill. When the dog's owner turns up dead, all hell breaks loose. It's all Walton can do to keep the two—no make that three—of them safe …

Find Book 26 here!
To find out more visit Dale Mayer's website.
https://geni.us/DMSWalton

Author's Note

Thank you for reading Baron: The K9 Files, Book 25! If you enjoyed the book, please take a moment and leave a short review.

Dear reader,

I love to hear from readers, and you can contact me at my website: www.dalemayer.com or at my Facebook author page. To be informed of new releases and special offers, sign up for my newsletter or follow me on BookBub. And if you are interested in joining Dale Mayer's Reader Group, here is the Facebook sign up page.
http://geni.us/DaleMayerFBGroup

Cheers,
Dale Mayer

About the Author

Dale Mayer is a *USA Today* best-selling author, best known for her SEALs military romances, her Psychic Visions series, and her Lovely Lethal Garden cozy series. Her contemporary romances are raw and full of passion and emotion (Broken But … Mending, Hathaway House series). Her thrillers will keep you guessing (Kate Morgan, By Death series), and her romantic comedies will keep you giggling (*It's a Dog's Life*, a stand-alone novella; and the Broken Protocols series, starring Charming Marvin, the cat).

Dale honors the stories that come to her—and some of them are crazy, break all the rules and cross multiple genres!

To go with her fiction, she also writes nonfiction in many different fields, with books available on résumé writing, companion gardening, and the US mortgage system. All her books are available in print and ebook format.

Connect with Dale Mayer Online

Dale's Website – www.dalemayer.com
Twitter – @DaleMayer
Facebook Page – geni.us/DaleMayerFBFanPage
Facebook Group – geni.us/DaleMayerFBGroup
BookBub – geni.us/DaleMayerBookbub
Instagram – geni.us/DaleMayerInstagram
Goodreads – geni.us/DaleMayerGoodreads
Newsletter – geni.us/DaleNews

www.ingramcontent.com/pod-product-compliance
Lightning Source LLC
Chambersburg PA
CBHW071434200726
48294CB00002B/631